"Can there be anything more wild and exciting than what we had, Taylor?"

The smoky quality of Jared's voice played across her frayed nerves, working its own magic on her senses. Before her mind's eye rose the image of his hard and superb physique, of his naked limbs entwined with hers, of strong, dark body hair grazing her softness.

No, she thought. Whatever else their marriage had lacked, it certainly hadn't lacked sensuality.

That he still wanted her was obvious—in the most primitive sense, at least. She could see it in those dark, dilated pupils. She closed her eyes against it now, knowing that he would recognize an answering and involuntary response in her if she let her guard down, and with the instinct of self-preservation she forced herself to remember....

ELIZABETH POWER was born in Bristol, England, where she still lives with her husband in a three-hundred-year-old cottage. A keen reader, as a teenager she had already made up her mind to be a novelist, although it wasn't until around age thirty that she took up writing seriously. Her love of nature and animals is reflected in a leaning toward vegetarianism. Good food and wine come high on her list of priorities, and what better way to sample these delights than by just having to take another trip to some new exotic resort? Oh, and, of course, to find a location for the next book...!

THE RUTHLESS MARRIAGE BID

ELIZABETH POWER

BLACKMAIL BRIDES

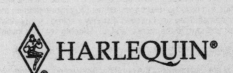
HARLEQUIN®

TORONTO • NEW YORK • LONDON
AMSTERDAM • PARIS • SYDNEY • HAMBURG
STOCKHOLM • ATHENS • TOKYO • MILAN • MADRID
PRAGUE • WARSAW • BUDAPEST • AUCKLAND

For Alan—as always.

ISBN 0-373-82033-X

THE RUTHLESS MARRIAGE BID

First North American Publication 2005.

www.eHarlequin.com

Printed in U.S.A.

CHAPTER ONE

HE WAS standing at the kerbside waiting to cross the road. It *was* him! Taylor thought chaotically, battling through the gathering dusk and the sheer volume of rush-hour traffic to catch another glimpse of that proud, dark head, of the striking height and self-assured stance that were unmistakably his.

She heard the rear door of the taxi slam behind her, heard Craig issuing instructions through the driver's window. But her mind and body were in turmoil, and as the taxi shot forward she swivelled round on her seat, scanning with blood-pumping anticipation, the busy street through the rear window.

The man was nowhere to be seen.

So she had just imagined him there, or been totally mistaken, she realised. As always.

Nervous tension dissipated beneath the familiar disappointment, the desolation that spread through her veins, as chilling as the late-winter afternoon. Beneath the thick grey overcoat she shivered, and was only warmed by the murmur of the infant waking in his car seat beside her, as the little starfish hand curled tightly around the finger that she readily proffered.

'You're a scamp,' she cooed at the appealingly chubby face beaming up at her from its knitted blue bonnet, but her finely drawn features, framed by a bob of gleaming brown, were etched with obvious tension.

She had been so sure it was him. She had even neglected to wave to Craig, she berated herself, still trying to shrug off the unsettling aftermath of mixed emotions fifteen minutes later when the taxi dropped her in the lamp-lit suburbs.

Still clutching her purse, with the baby seat suspended from her other hand, she started walking towards one of the high, Victorian villas.

A shadow fell across her path, large and ominous, and she gasped, dropping her purse, fear for the child she carried tightening her fingers around the handle of the little chair as the tall dark figure loomed from out of the shadows.

'Jared!'

'Hello, Taylor.' With one fluid movement, he stooped to pick up her purse, the long, dark overcoat he hadn't bothered to fasten spreading to remind her of a raven swooping to its prey, the hair that waved over his collar gleaming ebony beneath the streetlamp.

'So it *was* you.' Jared Steele. A leader in enterprises covering everything from finance to the highest technology. Thirty-eight years old, now, she calculated—twelve years older than she was. Rich, powerful and, as she had found out to her cost, unscrupulous.

Too stunned to thank him, her fingers closed around the rectangle of black leather he had retrieved for her. Her hands were shaking and she had to swallow to try and moisten her uncomfortably dry throat. 'Outside the studios. Crossing the road…' But he hadn't used the crossing. He must have flagged down a taxi… 'You followed me!' she breathed, annoyance surfacing with the over-riding excitement that made her pulses race, her legs go weak, which owed more to coming face to face with him like this than her first, initial dread of being mugged.

'I wanted to see you.'

'Why?'

He didn't answer and following his gaze to the little baby

seat, she realised suddenly what was going through his mind.

'You've been busy since I saw you last.'

Of course. What other conclusion could he have drawn?

'When was that?' she enquired pointedly, ignoring his hard unspoken question. In the eighteen months since that last bitter row he had never come looking for her. She wondered why he had decided to now.

He shrugged and, ignoring her in turn, said, 'I must confess this was the last thing I expected.' His mouth appeared chiselled out of granite as he dropped another glance to the sleeping infant. Those deep-set eyes were shielded by his dark and enviably long lashes, eyes that could reduce one to pulp with just one withering look, Taylor remembered, or evoke the most thrilling and dangerous thoughts in any woman under eighty. 'After all your protestations about having babies. What was it? An accident?' His voice, which had always had the power to arouse her with its smoky sexuality held a derisive edge and his breath rose in a warm cloud on the frosty air. 'We both know maternity wasn't on your agenda. Or perhaps it was just me you weren't partial to, not having children. That's one conclusion my ego's going to have to deal with, isn't it, Taylor?'

'Why?' His comments stabbed at her, opening old and painful wounds. 'Because I was so obviously instrumental in losing yours!'

His head seemed to jerk back as though she had laid a whip across his face. But if he was recoiling from such frank and blatant words, she thought, pushing angrily past him, perhaps he would know what it was like—how it had felt—when he had used them—and so mercilessly—on her.

'I must congratulate you. You've done well for yourself. Make-up artist—*and* with a top production company.' His voice lacked praise, his remarks only serving to let her know that it was no accident—this meeting; that he had actually been checking up on her. 'But then you always were ambitious, weren't you?' he said.

A little shiver ran through her from his chilling tone because, of course, they had argued about that too.

'And lover boy outside the studios.' He was right behind her, his deep voice insistent, taunting. 'Might I hazard a guess that he'd be the child's father?'

So he had seen her with Craig; noticed that affectionate kiss the man had given her as he had handed her into the taxi. Some deep emotional pain stopped her from immediately putting him straight.

'How terribly astute of you,' she breathed, hurting from the memory of the scarring rows that her miscarriage, if not wholly initiating, had only succeeded in exacerbating.

'Is he living here with you?' A toss of his chin indicated the three-storey house as he drew level with her along the short driveway.

'If you mean are we sleeping under the same roof...' Taylor forced herself to stay calm, keep her clear, mellow voice low as she reached the front door, put her key in the lock '...the answer's "yes."'

She didn't get to turn the key, her small gasp of shock the only emotion she allowed herself to show, as hard fingers on her wrist pulled her to face him. Under the stern glare of the security light his angular features looked grim and bloodless.

'Didn't it seem to matter to you that you're still married?' Eyes, as dark as night, seemed to pierce the depths of hers, boring into her from a mask of anger and disbelief. 'Didn't it ever occur to you to ask me for a divorce?'

Almost as tall as he was in her high-heeled boots, she could feel the warmth of his breath on her forehead, feel his anger beating against her like ravaging fire. But his nearness alone seemed to be stripping her of her self-possession, without the heat of his accusations that had she been in his shoes, she had to agree, she would have richly deserved. His accusations, however, only fuelled her own anger. Besides, Josh was growing fretful, sensing the insecurity of the situation, and forcibly she pulled herself free, saying, 'Why? I seem to remember you had no qualms about having a mistress and a wife!' She opened the front door now, flicked on a switch just inside.

Light spilled out, illuminating the wide Victorian hallway. It was cluttered with toys, boxes and coats and a baby buggy.

'Are you going to ask me in?'

For an answer she simply left the door open behind her, her shoulders stiffening beneath the stylish coat when she heard him close it, muting the growl of a car in the suburban road.

Without glancing back, she took the post she had picked up into the long, narrow kitchen, doing her best not to trip over the two yowling Siamese cats that had suddenly besieged her, vying for her attention, brown tails lightly flaying her calves.

Carefully, she set Josh down on the small sofa at one end of the narrow room, tossing aside a cushion, a shopping bag, a pile of folded garments, in need of ironing.

'Very domesticated.'

The deep drawl from behind her had her turning sharply.

Jared was standing in the doorway, looking, as his name suggested, like a man of steel. But with his hands rammed deep into his pockets, long legs planted firmly apart, he was too fine a male specimen for Taylor's eyes not to be drawn to the impeccable cut of the dark suit he wore under the long coat. With unsparing cruelty her gaze was dragged over the wide shoulders and the hard lean lines of his waist and hips and, as he stood there surveying the chaos of the cluttered kitchen with marked disdain curling his mouth, all she could think of was how it had felt to sink her nails into that broad, bare back while she had sobbed out his name...

The memory rocked her, threatening her equilibrium and, moving across to the fridge, in a less than steady voice she asked, 'Why did you want to see me?'

He came in then, every footstep measured, slow, precise.

'I don't think that takes too much working out.'

Wary green eyes clashed with darkest brown, her perfectly straight nose and softly tapered chin lifting as she opened the fridge, took out a tin of cat food. What was she supposed to deduce from that? Had the mysterious Alicia decided she had had enough of playing nursemaid to a husband she didn't love? Was she finally giving him up to be with Jared?

Pain cut deep, but she gritted her teeth.

The cats were going mad, particularly Thai, the male Siamese who was making his demands known now by clawing at her coat and yowling vociferously. On top of that, Josh had started to make his presence felt with small whimpers from the sofa, depriving her of the luxury of any self-pity.

Dumping the opened can of food down on the worktop, Taylor slid off her coat. Then wished she hadn't when she noticed the way Jared's gaze skimmed over her, taking in the willowy lines of her body beneath her cream polo-necked sweater and the full, bottle-green skirt that fell in soft folds over the spiked-heeled black boots.

'You've got thinner,' he observed, making no attempt to hide his blatant appraisal of her figure.

An insidious tension crept through her as she tossed her coat down on one of the high stools near the breakfast bar that Craig had made during one of his more adventurous DIY moments. Opening a drawer, she rummaged for a spoon, reached for the partially used can of cat food.

'I hardly think my weight's an issue here.' She stooped

to scoop the contents into the two bowls on the floor beside the breakfast bar. Two ravenous heads dived into them before she had even finished.

'I think it's very much an issue.' Those dark eyes were still assessing her, raking over her flushed features and the chic hair, now unintentionally tousled, as she straightened from her task. 'But then you were never much more than a reed at the best of times, were you?' he said, with an almost bored glance towards the cats who were putting on a show of not having eaten in weeks.

'If you say so.'

Josh's demands had replaced the cats' with his sudden persistent crying, and Taylor swung away to free him from the confines of his seat. His little face was red and crumpled. 'He needs feeding—and changing,' she noted as she lifted him up, her tone suddenly weary, the shock of this unexpected meeting with the man she had longed, yet half dreaded, to see again, taking its toll on her nerves.

'And you look as though you could do with some help.'

He was there beside her, too big, too awesome and far, far too close.

'I'm perfectly capable,' she returned with her voice cracking, and moved quickly away from him, wondering what he was thinking as he watched her carrying Josh across the kitchen. That the baby's hair, so close to hers, was almost the same rich brown? That Josh's wispy curls must have been inherited from his father since hers was so thick and sleek?

'As capable of wringing a man's heart?'

Taking the baby bottle out of the fridge, she met those dark eyes with a guarded question in her own. 'What?'

'How long was it, Taylor?'

'How long was what?' She slammed the fridge closed. Outside, in the hallway, she caught the sudden, unexpected sound of the front door being opened.

'How long before you jumped into another man's bed after leaving mine?'

Something flared in her eyes, locking her jaw tight. 'How dare you even ask that when—'

She bit back her words, her body stiffening from the footsteps moving along the hall, tension warring with anger inside of her. He had come here assuming the worst about her, and through a crazy desire to lash out at him she hadn't put him straight. Now she was torn between wishing she had and relishing his being taken down a peg when he realised that he had made a total fool of himself.

'Hello, Tay…' The young woman who had just come in stopped dead, her greeting curtailed by the sight of the tall man standing there in the kitchen.

'Jared! Jared Steele!' A year or two older than Taylor, Charity Lucas had a sparkling smile that seemed as wide now as her mane of short shaggy auburn hair. 'What on earth are you doing here?'

'Charity?' Jared's greeting was cordial, yet laced with puzzlement.

Though she was inches shorter than Taylor and totally dwarfed by Jared, Charity's ebullient personality seemed nonetheless to instantly fill the room. 'Do you two know each other?' Her words were strung with surprise as she looked from one to the other.

'You could say that.' Jared's tone was dry. 'And I could be forgiven for asking you the same thing?'

Charity laughed. 'Taylor rents from us. Upstairs. I'm her landlady.' She held out her arms to the baby who, ever since she had come in, had been making little noises of recognition and was now straining towards her. 'How's he been?'

'Fine.' Handing Josh over to the other woman, Taylor couldn't look at Jared, but she could sense clarity dawning on that sharp brain. 'Craig told me to tell you he'd be late tonight.'

She was too aware of Jared listening to every word, as conscious, no doubt, of her tense discomfort as he was of the other woman hugging and kissing the happy, gurgling Josh.

'I can do that now.' Taylor was disappointed when Charity readily took the baby bottle from her. She would have preferred to deal with the feed herself, desperate, at that moment, for something to do. 'You didn't tell me you knew Jared.'

Not sure what to do with her hands, now that she had nothing to hold, Taylor uttered an awkward little laugh, reaching for her coat. 'No.' She wondered how Charity knew him, but was too disconcerted to ask.

'Hardly a reflection on you, Charity.' Moving towards them with that lithe grace of his, on the surface Jared oozed irresistible charm. 'It seems she decided to keep us both in the dark,' he breathed with the flash of a smile. His eyes, though, pierced like rods of steel. There was a flush lying along his cheekbones that hinted at some fervent emotion, but one that vied with something like satisfaction that said he had the upper hand and was enjoying every minute of it.

'In what capacity do you two know each other?' Charity asked, balancing Josh on a curvy hip while she started to warm his bottle, adding laughingly, 'Or is that rather an indelicate question?'

Dark head tilted, Jared's eyes met Taylor's in penetrating enquiry. It was strange, she thought swallowing, how he had made all the wrong assumptions, and she was the one left feeling like a fool.

Her small breasts lifted as she caught her breath, wondering what to say. She hadn't told Charity she was married and she didn't want to spring the truth on her friend like this. And whether Jared was surprisingly sensitive to that fact, she wasn't sure, but swiftly he was answering, 'Let's just say we go back quite a way.'

'Really?' Bustling around the worktop, Charity sent an enquiring glance at each of them over her shoulder, bouncing Josh on her arm as he suddenly started crying again. But then obviously sensing that she was treading on uneven ground, quickly she went on, 'Jared's a friend and business associate of Dad's. I met him first when I came home one hols from university and he was staying with them, and in those days I must admit to having had a glorious crush on him.' The contentment and security in her marriage gave Charity the freedom to declare it so openly, Taylor realised, although the hint of colour in the woman's cheeks assured her that where Jared Steele was concerned, even the most fulfilled of women weren't entirely immune. 'Will you let me make him some tea? Or are you keen to have him all to yourself? Take him upstairs?'

Exchanging glances with Jared, Taylor clung to her coat as though to a protective shield.

'Well?' she asked, hoping he wouldn't accept Charity's offer, yet wanting to delay the inevitability of being alone with him again.

'I think,' he said, dropping a glance at Thai who, having wolfed down his meal, suddenly shot out of the room as if he'd been startled by some unseen horror, 'tea would be very nice—some other time. But right now Taylor and I do have things to discuss.'

Do we? she thought, watching the smaller, more subdued Asia delicately picking at her food, and feeling something like cold desolation trickling through her. Surely there could be only one thing he would want to discuss after the tumultuous peaks and troughs that had been their marriage?

'I'll look in before I leave,' he promised Charity, before

Taylor guided him back into the hall and up the stairs leading to the top floor.

'So the cats aren't yours. The baby isn't yours. And your
lover's somebody else's!' he comprehended as soon as he
was in her flat. There was a marked silence about the place
after all the domesticity downstairs.

'I never said anyone was my lover! Unlike you, I do
have some respect for other people's marriages!' she flung
at him, tense from the effort of trying to stay in control.

The hard masculine face was etched with some harsh
emotion and anger darkened his eyes to slits of jet, but he
said nothing.

'I work with Craig,' Taylor continued then, 'and he took
Josh to the studios today because Charity's mother had a
fall and needed her there. You saw us together and just
assumed what you wanted to. Like you were so quick to
assume that Josh was mine!' she accused, tossing her coat
over the back of one of a pair of matching sofas which,
though in immaculate order, she had managed to pick up
cheaply at a clearance auction.

'A natural deduction, in the circumstances,' Jared muttered, 'as I think you'll agree.' He was standing in the middle of the impeccably furnished room, looking around him,
and even its generous proportions couldn't detract from his
magnificence, or that air of innate authority that was as
much a part of him as his shadow. 'I should have known
better, shouldn't I? Somehow that delightfully homely
scene downstairs didn't quite gel with my memory of the
girl I knew.' His gaze was still raking over her carefully
chosen belongings; over the sparse but tasteful ornaments
and co-ordinating pictures, the flawless rugs and sofas and
the low-level bookcases with their immaculate veneer.
'Now this is more like it,' he breathed heavily, making her
wonder what he was thinking because, after the domestic
chaos to which he had just referred below, the flat only

seemed to emphasise the ordered isolation of her own existence. 'This is much more in keeping with the Taylor Steele I knew. Or is it back to Taylor Adams now?' He didn't need to ask if she was using her maiden name. If she hadn't been, then Charity might have guessed the truth. 'Why didn't you tell her you were married?' he demanded with some unfathomable emotion burning like dark fire in his eyes.

She shrugged. 'The question never came up.'

As she made to move past him, hard fingers closed around her upper arm. 'It just did.'

He looked so angry that beneath the pale sweater, Taylor shivered. 'I don't know.' Disconcerted, she pulled herself out of his grasp.

In truth, she hadn't told her friend and landlady—or indeed anyone who didn't need to know—that she had been married—and certainly not that her marriage had broken up. She didn't like the sense of personal failure it implied.

She went across to the window, drew the heavy curtains before turning back to him. 'You said we had things to discuss.'

'We most certainly have.'

Tension coiled in her stomach. 'Like what?'

He didn't answer for a moment. Then in that deep authoritative way of his he advised, 'Sit down, Taylor.'

An ache seemed to start somewhere in the middle of her chest as she did as he suggested, dropping down onto one of the sofas. It was her flat, yet even here he was the one giving the orders, the one in control, she acknowledged grudgingly, when he remained firmly on his feet.

'I know we made a hash of our marriage. And I can see you've picked yourself up...' he sent another glance around the room '...sorted your life out quite admirably. It almost makes a man feel...superfluous, especially when all the funds paid into your account were returned in full.'

'What did you think I'd do, Jared? Take it all with un-
dying gratitude? Did you think I wouldn't be able to manage on my own?'

'I didn't *think* anything. I didn't want you to have to—
manage, as you put it—or to experience any unnecessary
difficulty. Not when I could make life easier for you, even
if you weren't living under my roof any more.'

'Well...as you can see...' a small gesture indicated the
modest comfort of the flat '...I'm not exactly living in
squalor or abject poverty.' Returning her gaze to his, she
wished she hadn't when the dark penetration of his eyes
sent a weakening torrent of emotion through her. Quietly,
through lips that seemed not to want to move, she murmured, 'Why have you come?'

The broad, masculine chest lifted and stilled as though
it were an effort for him to say what he had come to say.
Behind him, the large mirror over the Victorian fireplace
reflected wide shoulders that were as rigid as iron.

'I don't know about you but...well this state of affairs...
It's hardly very satisfactory, is it? I mean...you living
here...while I...' He glanced away from her, his teeth
clenched, as though the state of affairs, as he had called it,
fuelled his anger. 'Being separated, yet not being free either. I think we should change things,' he rasped.

The composure Taylor prided herself on had deserted her
somewhere between coming up here and when he had told
her to sit down, and now her words left her on a low croak.
'Change things?'

Again there was hesitation in Jared's usually arrogant
manner. 'We can't go on like this,' he stated with an air of
finality. 'I certainly don't think it an ideal situation. And
I'm sure you can't think so. This may come as a surprise
to you, but I miss the domestic scene. Call me crazy if you
like but I'm keen to throw myself right back there into

matrimonial bliss—have a second stab at it—but as you can appreciate, I can't do it without your co-operation.'

What was he saying? That he wanted them to try again? Surprise, shock and an emotion to which she wanted to give no credence surged through her. Was he saying he had missed her? That he still wanted her?

Well of course he did, an inner little voice told her cruelly after the initial shock of his statement began to wear off. Hadn't he had the best of both worlds while they had been together?

Slamming the lid on a well of anguished memories, she asked tentatively, 'Are you implying we should get back together?' But then the ambiguity of his statement suddenly struck her, making her tag on, 'Or are you asking me for a divorce?' She was relieved that no emotion crept into her voice, giving away how much he still affected her and, sparing herself the humiliation of a possible rejection, quickly she added, 'Because if you are, I don't intend standing in your way.'

Was it relief or surprise, she wondered, that brought him down onto the opposite sofa? That furrowed his brow and kept his voice low and husky when he spoke again? 'I hadn't realised you'd agree to one so readily.'

Taylor drew in a breath that was almost too painful to expel. And to think she could so easily have misunderstood!

She gave a careless movement of her shoulder. 'Why not? We're living separate lives. You said so yourself.' So he wanted to get married again. Have a second stab at it, as he had so casually and unthinkingly called it. 'Who is she?' she asked caustically. 'The wonderful Alicia?'

'*What?*' His eyes had narrowed into slits.

'This woman you're prepared to sacrifice your freedom to for a second time?'

He was still looking at her as though he were trying to

fathom out why she was asking. Or, from the grimness of his mouth, perhaps he thought she had no right to question him on the subject—no right at all.

'Or have you found someone else?' Jumping up, bitterly she couldn't help flinging down at him, 'Someone else willing to give you the children I couldn't—no, *wouldn't*—agree to?'

Frighteningly swift, Jared was on his feet. 'You haven't a clue what you're saying,' he rasped in a harshly chiding tone. 'I was hoping by now you would have grown up a little and come to your senses! You're still governed by that jealous nature and a far too vivid imagination. As for children—that isn't important.'

'No?' Her thick hair moved sleekly as she tilted her head, her green eyes dark and injured. 'Funny! It seemed of paramount importance when you were married to me!'

She gave a small cry as he suddenly reached out, dragging her against him, the hands gripping her upper arms, hard and bruising.

'I still am. Married to you,' he breathed, his strong white teeth clamping together, his jaw, with that marked cleft at its centre, locked in anger and some other, more primal emotion that excited as much as it unnerved her.

His closeness could have been her undoing. The strength of those arms that held her but a few centimetres from his body, his familiar, elusive scent and the latent power of his sexuality all combined to make her head swim with the longing to throw her arms around him, tilt her lips in shameless invitation to his. But common sense prevailed and beneath the burn of his gaze she taunted in a whisper and with a control she was far from feeling, 'Do you want both of us, Jared?'

His features were almost feral, nostrils flaring, his eyes glittering with something that for a few heady seconds had Taylor panicking, fearing that he was going to take the decision away from her and plunge them both into a moment's savage passion of the kind that had ruled them both during the final days of their marriage. A passion that now they would only both regret.

But then suddenly, and with a heavy lifting of his chest, as if it had taken every ounce of will-power he possessed, he released her.

'I'll be in touch,' he muttered breathlessly, and a few seconds later she heard his footsteps thundering down over the stairs.

CHAPTER TWO

'YOUR *husband*!' Charity breathed, having called to ask if Taylor could spare a carton of milk later that evening. 'Why didn't you ever tell me? No, don't answer that,' she added quickly, palms upwards in negation of any explanation that might be forthcoming. 'It's none of my business and you have a right to keep it to yourself.'

With anyone else, Taylor thought, it might have been a prompt for more information, but she knew that with Charity that wasn't the case. Just as she knew that the request for milk wasn't a ploy to question her about Jared. Taylor had offered the information voluntarily and with little prompting. Besides, with a family and two cats to feed, Charity was always running out of milk.

'I'm just not too proud of carrying around the stigma of a broken marriage,' Taylor admitted, reaching into the fridge for the small, unopened carton.

'Oh, Taylor! It's hardly a stigma these days.'

'Well, a failure then.'

Charity treated her to one of her caring smiles. 'Not even that. It's because you do everything so perfectly. Always look good. Manage a career and—' she sent a glance around the modestly fitted but pristine kitchen '—somehow keep your home spick and span. Thanks.' She took the carton Taylor handed her, giving it a shake as she said wryly, 'Never running out of basic necessities. Sometimes you've got to realise that you're human too. It's all right not to succeed in everything.'

Was that how Charity—and possibly other people—saw

her? Taylor wondered, shocked. As a kind of superwoman? The proverbial perfectionist?

Closing the fridge, she gave her a friend a half-hearted smile. She wasn't sure she liked being viewed like that at all.

'Are you going to at least let me in on how long you've known him?' the other woman ventured.

She owed Charity that at least, Taylor decided, having deceived her over her marital status even if it were only by omission, although she had gone as far as to tell both Charity and Craig that she had had a relationship that hadn't worked out.

'It was four and a half years ago,' Taylor told her, opening the dishwasher to unload it, releasing a sudden cloud of steam. 'I was working in a small provincial theatre as assistant to the set designer. I think Jared knew the leading lady of the play we were putting on at the time. His mother had been an actress and I suppose he knew people through her. Anyway, the theatre was in extreme financial difficulty and was scheduled for closure at the end of that season.' Carefully she stacked several small plates in the cupboard above the worktop. 'It had been a theatre for ninety years and was going to mean a great loss to the community. I found out later that Jared financed it, prevented it from closing down.

'One of the cast threw a party and that was the first time I saw him. All he did was look at me across the room...' And she had been lost for ever, a helpless, willing slave to his enthralling sexuality.

She stared wistfully down at her hand as though seeing something more than the little warm glass she had used for her fruit juice that morning.

At twenty-one she had been a virgin, green and untutored in the mysteries of love and passion, wary after the unsettled nature of her parents' marriage.

There had been a few hard years before then, unhappy years when, after losing the father she had adored, she had gone to live with her mother and step-father. Almost immediately, however, she had been made to feel like an interloper. Her mother had made a new life for herself that didn't take account of looking after a lonely, spirited teenager. As soon as she had been old enough, Taylor had left home, working hard to put herself through art college. Before she was even nineteen, her mother emigrated to Australia and, all alone in the world, Taylor had studied single-mindedly, shrugging off all advances by the opposite sex, except the most innocent and undemanding of dates.

Jared, though, had become her lover almost from the start. By that time her career was already under way. Not that it would have mattered, she reflected poignantly, forgetting for a few moments that Charity was there, because the passions that had ravaged them had been too great for denial or restraint.

Within a month she had moved out of her bedsit into his luxury penthouse apartment. And two months after that, just after her twenty-second birthday, they were married on a Hawaiian beach, pledging their vows to the soughing breezes and the song of an azure ocean.

She had invited her mother to attend, sending two airline tickets and a hotel booking with the simple invitation, which had been politely declined. Even that, however, hadn't detracted from the magic of her wedding day.

It had been a partnership made in heaven—or so she had thought—until the party Jared had thrown a few weeks afterwards to celebrate their marriage, to introduce his friends and business associates to his new wife.

With few friends of her own, Taylor had invited just one or two people with whom she had been working at the theatre and, still basking in the warmth of being Jared's new bride, was enjoying herself enormously at that party.

It was only when, somewhat overwhelmed by all their con-
gratulations and good wishes, she had wandered out onto
the balcony that surrounded the penthouse that she had
heard the two women talking.

One voice she instantly recognised as that of the leading
lady of the play that had just finished running, the other
belonged to an older woman she hadn't met until that night.

Obscured by a screen of metal lacework supporting a
thick and prolific vine, Taylor had stopped, hesitant to ven-
ture further, suddenly aware of the nature of the women's
conversation.

'It's been so quick,' the familiar voice was saying. 'I'd
never have labelled Jared as the impulsive type. But you
could have knocked me down with a feather when he came
back from Hawaii married. I mean, after... What was the
name of that woman he was seeing in Philadelphia?
Alicia?' And after a murmur of uncertainty, 'Oh, I know it
was an impossible situation,' that same voice continued,
'but well...he was *so* involved.'

'A woman with a disabled husband she's never going to
leave doesn't exactly make for a settled future,' the older
woman responded, 'and I suppose Jared couldn't wait
around forever. He's a full-blooded male. He needs a
wife—children—and when all is said and done, well...
she's a lovely little thing.'

'Hardly little!' the leading lady contradicted with emphasis. 'She almost matches him in height—certainly in
those heels!'

'Yes, but she's so much younger than he is, that's what
I meant,' the other woman elaborated. 'This...Alicia, I believe, was much nearer his age. Still, he's certainly picked
one young enough and ripe enough to have his babies. She
looks as though she'll conceive every time he sneezes! And
what with being so willowy and vulnerable looking—no

wonder he couldn't resist her! She must bring out the protective instinct in him!'

They both laughed, a muted sound drifting out across the
dark waters of the Thames and the fairy-lit city.

Unable to face them, numbly Taylor had retreated inside.

When she had challenged Jared later about his being involved with a married woman, his reply had been surprisingly curt.

'Who have you been talking to?' he had wanted to know,
flinging open the door to the wardrobe.

'It was just something I overheard,' she said.

He had sworn under his breath when she repeated her
question.

'She was separated from her husband when I met her.
He had a car accident and she went back to him. That's all
there was to it,' he said.

But it wasn't, Taylor thought, seeing in that strong
face—absorbed as he unfastened a cuff-link—an unmistak-
able tension that spoke volumes.

'Did you want to marry her?' she had asked tentatively,
to which he responded only with, 'I married you.'

'Did you love her?' She hadn't intended to ask him so
directly, nor had he been expecting her to, she reflected,
forever afterwards hearing those hard and angry words he
had lobbed back at her.

'Yes I loved her. Are you satisfied? I had an affair. It's
something I'm not proud of, but it happened. Now let's
forget it,' he had seethed through gritted teeth, before
storming out of the bedroom.

Which was easier said than done, Taylor thought now,
because she had tried. Nevertheless, the doubts and anxieties had seeded themselves in her mind, causing unnecessary tensions between them, sprouting up with renewed
vigour every time he went away. The situation wasn't
helped when sometimes, answering the phone, she heard

the line go dead at the other end, or when someone ringing from his office innocently asked her if she knew when his flight would be in from Philadelphia. He had told her he was going to New York, and that, she knew, was the truth, but he hadn't mentioned going on to Philadelphia. So why had he kept it from her? she had asked herself, too aware that Philadelphia was where this Alicia lived. Why, unless he had had some very strong reason to feel guilty about it?

Unsure of him, plagued by long-buried insecurities, she had thrown herself wholeheartedly into her job, her mind made up about one thing.

She would never have children. Never entertain bringing babies into a marriage that wasn't one hundred per cent secure.

When Jared had suggested starting a family, she had told him she wanted to wait—that she wasn't that bothered about having children at all. Keen for an heir to succeed him in the company he had built single-handed, it was then, after several attempts on his part to change her mind had failed, that he had accused her of being interested only in her career.

'And what's wrong with that?' she had flung at him, remembering all too painfully that conversation on the balcony, adding that if he had just got married to have children, then he should have married someone who would have happily provided him with them.

Angrily then, he had tossed back, 'I thought I had!'

So that was it, she had thought, broodingly, watching as he poured himself a Scotch and soda in the apartment's luxurious sitting room, challenging him with, 'Is that the only reason for our marriage?'

'Don't be so stupid,' he had said coldly.

But the doubts and resentments had festered and grown. After that, whenever he broached the subject, she would simply clam up.

She couldn't—wouldn't! she'd assured herself, agree to have what might possibly turn out to be a tug-of-war child, not when she was so convinced that at any moment he might leave her for the woman he really loved.

When she had accidentally conceived, fears for her child's future had made her anxious and uncommunicative, something to which Jared had been acutely sensitive, even if not to the reason why.

'Perhaps this is what this marriage needs,' he had stressed one evening, a couple of months into her pregnancy.

'What?' she had challenged. 'Something to keep me in my place while you go off anytime and anywhere you please?' Already battling with irresolvable insecurities, it hadn't helped when he had told her in no uncertain terms to grow up.

With their relationship already floundering, he had flown off to the States for a conference with several of his American company's hi-tech whiz-kids a couple of days afterwards, during which time Taylor had started to miscarry. When he returned ten days later, her pregnancy was over.

'Well, that's exactly what you wanted, wasn't it?' he said when, still numb and wretched with grief she told him she had lost the baby. He had looked, she'd thought—wondering if he had had a particularly gruelling conference—bleak-eyed, yet frighteningly grim.

Illogically blaming herself for losing her baby, wanting to hurt herself as well as to hurt Jared, not thinking straight, she had thrown back, 'Oh, sure! I arranged for it to happen! Well, you were having such a good time with your mistress, weren't you? Why not!'

His eyes were glittering with such intense anger she wondered now what had prevented him from actually hitting her as he had snarled back, 'At least she wouldn't sacrifice

a child for her precious job!' There was such an edge of
steel to his voice that she knew that whatever feeling he
might have had for her, until then, she had killed with that
last rash retort.

It was, however, to Taylor, an admission that he was still
involved with the other woman, and one that had propelled
her into leaving. The very next morning after he had left
for his office, she had scribbled him a note, laid her wedding ring on top of it and fled, and she hadn't seen him
again until today.

'Mmm,' Charity murmured expressively, jolting Taylor
out of her painful retrospection.

'Mmm, what?' she pressed, agitated, quickly stowing
away the glass she was still holding.

'Just "Mmm,"' the woman responded, as Taylor turned
round again. She could feel her friend's perceptive gaze
resting on her flushed cheeks.

Craig was home and from the floor below she could hear
water running in the pipes, caught the strains of one of his
country CDs playing. Safe, homely Craig who liked nothing better than to be with his family, to put up a shelf and
play the odd game of golf when his job as lighting technician allowed.

'I suppose a man like Jared could be quite overwhelming
to be married to,' Charity expressed as though picking up
on Taylor's thoughts. 'Forceful. Possessive. Exciting. I
know I said I had a crush on him but if he had asked me
out, I'd have been scared to death! I mean all that dyna-
mism and vitality! And the sophistication that makes the
hard-headedness behind it all so scary and...I don't
know... I don't suppose I should say it to you but, well...
thrilling!'

Charity's eyes were bright from the teenage fantasies she
must have woven over what was after all an acquaintance
of her parents while she studied Taylor sagaciously, looking

no doubt for some flicker of agreement in her friend. But all Taylor said dryly was, 'And with a temper to match,' because of course Jared Steele was all of those things.

'Ah-ah,' Charity breathed. 'I wondered why he came down those stairs like a bolt of lightning without calling in on his way out as he promised.'

In one of the rooms below, Josh had suddenly started to cry.

'He's just the sort of man I would have picked for you, Taylor.' Charity was already moving towards the door. 'I'm sorry it didn't work out.'

Taylor gave an outwardly nonchalant shrug. 'We had our differences.'

'With no chance that the two of you will ever get back together?' Charity looked hopeful, but Taylor shook her head.

'No,' she answered, her lowered lashes concealing the pain in her eyes as she thought of their bitter arguments, remembered the conversation she had had with Jared earlier. 'No,' she said again, more adamantly this time. 'No chance at all.'

Taylor was putting the finishing touches to the face of the young actress who was last on the set that morning. It was for a televised play and the outside shooting had been completed two weeks ago. Now it was just a matter of finishing the studio shots and, taking a break, several members of the cast and production team who had wandered into Makeup were sitting around, chatting and drinking coffee.

'...didn't think when I arranged to pick them up at lunchtime that they'll be defrosted by the time I get them home.'

One of the production assistants was bemoaning her stupidity over some desserts she had bought for dinner. Concentrating on blending blusher across the young actress's cheeks, Taylor wasn't really listening until she heard her own name mentioned.

'Just give them to Taylor to hold for the afternoon,' Paul Salisbury was advising dryly. 'That should keep them frozen.'

Tall and blond, Paul was a brilliant photographer who believed his prowess with women was all due to his good looks and his success with a camera. With Taylor, however, he had had his grand opinion of himself sadly shattered, she realised, when she had refused to go out with him—or with any man, she had determined bitterly, even if she weren't still married—which was why, she decided, Paul had been sniping at her ever since.

'I'll have you know, Taylor is a very warm and sensitive person,' Craig Lucas, mug in hand, perched on the edge of a table, lobbed back.

Dear unassuming Craig, Taylor thought, sharing a smile with the man with twinkling brown eyes, whose tawny head was bent slightly forward—as though he were uncomfortable with his long lean frame, she had often thought— grateful for the unnecessary but caring way he had leaped to her defence.

He was, however, looking towards the door, just as everyone else was and, glancing curiously over her shoulder, Taylor stifled a small shocked gasp.

'How—how did you get in here?' she stammered, her pulses quickening under the dark brooding gaze of the man who had just come through the doorway. Security was stringent and no one could get in without a pass.

'I told them who I was and that I wanted to see you,' Jared answered casually.

And that would have been enough, with that daunting air of authority and that core-hard confidence, Taylor thought grudgingly, to overcome the hardest obstacles.

She saw the withering glance he directed at Craig and

wondered if he had heard the technician's complimentary remarks about her; heard what Paul had said. She couldn't help noticing though how the long dark coat and immaculate dark suit seemed to give Jared an edge over the younger men, over the rest of the production team and over her, dressed as she was, like they all were, in casual sweaters and jeans.

As if on an unspoken order, the others were already trooping out.

'There,' Taylor said, having made a great show of ignoring him by brushing powder from the girl's cheeks and standing back at last to examine her work. 'Now go out there and do your best.'

Getting to her feet, the actress scarcely glanced at her reflection, concentrating only on sending Jared a blatantly inviting smile before leaving them to join the others.

Disconcerted at being alone with him, Taylor began tidying her cosmetics, discarding used tissues, fastening lids on jars.

'I take it you came here to discuss…what we were talking about the other day.' Somehow she couldn't bring herself to say the word 'divorce'. It hurt enough to realise that he hadn't wasted any time in getting back to her. But that was pride, she told herself. Nothing more. 'If that's the case…' she was tossing brushes into a tall plastic holder '…I hardly think we can talk here.'

'Exactly,' that deep voice agreed. 'Which is why I've booked lunch for us both in a quiet little restaurant I know, so if you'd like to get your coat, we can be on our way.'

'Now wait a minute!' Slamming down a pot of cleansing cream in front of the brightly lit mirror, Taylor faced him with her arms folded, supported by the shelf below the bank of mirrors that stretched along one wall. 'Aren't you rather jumping the gun just a bit? What makes you think I can just drop everything and follow you like some obedient little pet dog?'

'Your receptionist—or whoever it was I spoke to when I telephoned earlier. She said you were doing your last job of the morning and that you'd probably be finished within half an hour.'

'Oh, did she?' Swinging back to her task, Taylor opened a drawer, dropped a few items into it and slammed it closed again. 'Well, I've got news for you, Jared. I still can't come with you.' There was a defiant air to her fine features as she delivered with just a shade of smugness, 'I've got a dental appointment first thing this afternoon.'

'Which is also why I booked a restaurant no more than ten minutes from the dental practice.'

'You...' Leaning back against the shelf again, Taylor wrapped her arms around herself in a subconsciously protective gesture, the bright lights behind her making her hair gleam like liquid silk as she shook her head. 'I don't believe you're for real,' she whispered, flabbergasted, feeling her privacy being sorely invaded. 'What rights have you got to go checking up on me? Are you hoping to find some besotted lover so you can sue *me* for adultery rather than admit to it yourself?'

A nerve seemed to jerk in his jaw, but he made no comment in response to her little outburst.

'It was more a case of serendipity than purposely checking up on you,' he said phlegmatically instead. 'When I phoned here they said that if I wanted to catch you I'd have to do so quickly as you had a dental appointment at two. I then deduced that you were probably using the same practice as when we were living together, so I simply rang and asked if my wife had arrived yet and when they told me when you were expected, I knew I'd guessed correctly.'

He had also assumed—and correctly—that for convenience she would still be using her married name at the dental practice. Silently she had to compliment him on his ingenuity, but his calculated determination unsettled her.

'And if I needed to find someone besotted...' Coolly he reached over her shoulder, causing her to catch her breath from his unsettling nearness as he flicked the switch that turned off the lights around the mirror. 'I don't think I'd need look much further than these studios, Taylor, do you?'

The meal was a tense, uneasy affair. At least where she was concerned, Taylor decided, which was why she had ordered only a piece of crisp bread with a light topping which she would still have had difficulty swallowing if it hadn't been for the mineral water she had ordered with it.

Jared, however, seemed perfectly relaxed as he tucked into his steak sandwich with a second cup of coffee. She supposed under normal circumstances she would have complimented him upon his choice of restaurant. Totally informal, it was small but airy, the tables well spaced, the efficient service apparent as soon as they stepped inside, when a waiter had swiftly and discreetly borne their coats away.

'No wonder you're so thin.' His dark glittering irises surveyed her with unmasked disapproval across the table. 'Charity's cats eat more than you do and they're like waifs. How long have you lived with Charity?' he was demanding before she could respond to his comments about her weight.

'I'm not living with them,' she stated pointedly.

'Don't split hairs,' he said, sounding impatient. 'You know exactly what I mean.'

Taylor inhaled deeply. He was right. It was pointless deliberately antagonising him. It was just that he hadn't even skirted the subject he had brought her out here to discuss and her anticipation had become a tight knot in her stomach.

'Just over a year,' she told him then. 'Within a week or two of my being engaged by the studios. With Josh on the way, Craig and Charity decided it would be practical financially to let the top floor. I was looking for a flat. And that was it. I couldn't have found anywhere better if I'd tried. Charity's such a lovely person it wasn't difficult striking up an instant friendship with her, and Craig's so easygoing, it's never been a problem working with him all day and seeing him socially as well. He's been a marvellous friend to me too.'

'Well, bully for Craig,' he drawled.

His meal finished, he was sitting with one elbow resting on the back of his chair, so that a good deal of white shirt was exposed beneath his open jacket.

Disconcertedly, Taylor dragged her gaze from the dark shadow of his body hair, clearly visible through the fine cotton, aware of a different kind of tension invading her now.

'You're determined not to like him, aren't you?' she accused, wondering for a few fleeting moments if his motive sprang from jealousy. But, no, she decided, dismissing the thought before it had scarcely taken shape. Jared Steele was the type of man who evoked that emotion in others, not experienced himself. And, anyway, he was in love with someone else. He had always loved someone else... 'I thought Charity was a friend of yours,' she challenged when he ignored her last question.

'She is. Or rather, her parents are.'

'Well, then,' Taylor uttered, with an unconscious lifting of her chin. 'Don't you think they—and she—might take exception to your insinuations that I'm having an affair with her husband? Because she's my friend too—and *I* do!'

A faint smile played around the hard masculine mouth. He didn't look at all perturbed.

'You've grown more confident,' he remarked.

His soft observation was unexpected and disarming and

quickly she lifted her glass, took a last draught of the cool water.

'What did you expect?' she challenged, setting her glass down on the pale cloth. 'Even the most naïve of us grow up—if we're forced to. And boy! Was I naïve!'

He acknowledged this only with a subtle lifting of a dark eyebrow.

'As I recall, you also didn't always make friends so easily. Or perhaps it was just that you didn't try.'

No, she thought. She always had been a bit of a loner, too shy and self-conscious for her own good. Even at school she had preferred to read or sketch rather than join in with the more communal pursuits of her peers. Perhaps that was just how she was. Or perhaps it sprang from a reluctance to get too close to anyone…

'We all change—for better or worse,' she said without thinking, and felt a sudden sharp emotion stab her.

She saw a furrow crease the high, intellectual forehead, met those far too perceptive eyes and looked quickly away.

'So what were you doing for the first six months after you ran away? I did contact your mother but she couldn't give me any information, and with no friends to pump—or relatives in this country—it proved to be an impossible task trying to find you.'

Had he looked for her? The knowledge brought a treacherous colour to her cheeks.

'It doesn't matter now, does it?' she murmured. After all, whatever his reason for trying to find her then, it didn't alter the fact that now he had found her, it was with only one purpose in mind. Which suited her fine! she convinced herself, in spite of the dull ache under her ribs.

He sat forward then, resting his elbows on the table, his chin on his clasped fingers.

'Humour me,' he breathed.

So she did, telling him how she had moved north for a

while, taking a short, intensive art course to further the basic grounding she had received at college. It was difficult though, keeping her voice steady, trying not to notice how strongly chiselled his face was, how his long lashes seemed to emphasise the darkness of his eyes and how his cruel mouth—a mouth that had once worked magic on her sensitive flesh—firmed now first with something like disapproval then with what...? Admiration? she wondered. Surely not!

'I saw an opening for a make-up artist down here in London, grabbed it and moved back. So there you have it. My wild and exciting life in its most uncensored form.'

A contemplative smile touched his lips. 'Can there be anything more wild and exciting than what we had, Taylor?'

The smoky quality of his voice played across her frayed nerves, working its own magic on her senses. Before her mind's eye rose the image of his hard and superb physique, of his naked limbs entwined with hers, of strong, dark body hair grazing her softness.

No, she thought. Whatever else their marriage had lacked, it certainly hadn't lacked sensuality.

That he still wanted her was obvious, in the most primitive sense at least. She could see it in those dark, dilated pupils, in the flaring of those proud nostrils that spoke of the huge hunting male catching the scent of a mate. She closed her eyes against it now, knowing that he would recognise an answering and involuntary response in her if for one moment she let her guard down, and with the instinct of self-preservation she forced herself to remember why he had come. Shakily she whispered, 'If you try to press a settlement on me, I'd like you to know, I won't accept it.'

When she looked at him again his heavy eyelids had come down over his eyes, cloaking any traces of desire. Grimness compressed his lips now and there was an unfathomable edge to his voice as he said, 'We'll talk about that later. In the meantime…' he dropped a glance to the gold wristwatch peeping out from his immaculate cuff '…I think you'd better get yourself sorted out for your dental appointment.'

He had left the car in a nearby Pay and Display car park, a newer model of the type of low-slung saloon he had always driven.

The wind was biting as they crossed the tarmac towards it.

'I thought spring was coming,' Taylor remarked, struggling to keep her coat from being wrenched open by the tugging wind. She felt low and dispirited, seeing the turn in the weather as a reflection of how her life had suddenly changed over the past week.

On the surface, nothing was different. She and Jared were still living apart. She still had her job. Her interests. Her friends. But seeing him again had revived memories she didn't want to think about; feelings she didn't want to feel. Oh, if only he had stayed away! If only things could have stayed the same and she could have gone on with her life thinking…

Thinking what? That one day he might come and tell her that he missed her? Loved her?

'What's wrong, Taylor?'

Of course, he had always been able to pick up on her mood, even if sometimes he had misinterpreted—and grossly—exactly what she was feeling.

'I was only thinking…' Suddenly her stomach muscles were knotting painfully again. 'What has today achieved, Jared? I mean, we haven't talked about anything we couldn't have said on the phone.'

He stopped abruptly, the speed of his action as he swung to face her making her recoil.

'What do you want me to say? Here are the blasted papers? Sign them. Thank you and goodbye!' His coat was flapping open, but he didn't seem to notice. Obviously he didn't feel the cold as she did, she thought, although his face looked taut, the skin stretched almost to transparency over his cheekbones, as though he weren't totally unaffected by the ravaging wind. 'Well, this might surprise you, Taylor, but that isn't why I insisted on seeing you today. It isn't my intention to sue for a divorce.' And then, after the briefest hesitation: 'I think we should get back together,' he said.

CHAPTER THREE

SHE looked at him quickly, her eyes dark and disbelieving, her heart beating so fast she felt faint.

'Why?' she whispered, that one syllable strung with all the pain and suspicion she had endured throughout her short marriage.

'Because I think it's what we both want,' he answered.

'And what about...your mistress?' It was a soft accusation over the sound of a van pulling out of the car park. 'What will she have to say about it?'

'There isn't any...*mistress*, as you call it. I told you—it was over between Alicia and me before we were ever married. But you refused to believe me.'

'Because of the way you were—the way you looked!— every time her name was mentioned.'

'That was in your mind.'

'Was it?' She regarded him obliquely, green eyes tortured and accusing. 'And I suppose those late-night phone calls from her were all in my mind!'

His skin seemed to blanch, and if that wasn't an admission of guilt, what was? she thought bitterly, seeing the disbelief in his eyes, the tightening line of his mouth.

'Did she...speak to you?' Caution marked his words and his slanted appraisal of her.

'No, she obviously didn't expect me to be there! Just like I didn't expect you to be in Philadelphia with her when you said you were going to New York!'

'I was in New York,' he stated bluntly, having no difficulty remembering the time to which she had referred. 'I had an unscheduled stopover in Philadelphia to visit a sick client who couldn't get to the main meeting. I didn't think it was worth mentioning—particularly as I knew what graphic pictures that imaginative little brain of yours could come up with. OK. Maybe I wasn't being entirely open with you...'

'Not open with me! That's an understatement!' she breathed, still raw from the memory of his deception.

'Taylor...'

As he took a step towards her she shrank back, shaking her head. 'No,' she murmured, denying him the right to hurt her for a second time, denying them both a second chance, though it was excruciating when all she longed to do was accede to his suggestion, throw herself like the helpless fool she had been back into his arms.

'And that's it?'

'That's it.'

'With not even a backward glance?' Some emotion she could have mistaken for pain had she not known him better clouded those beautiful eyes. He shook his head. 'Without any regret? Surely, I would have thought that even you—'

He broke off, hearing the sound that had also caught Taylor's attention. It was the pitiable crying of a small child.

She couldn't have been more than three or four, Taylor realised, horrified, as the little girl wandered out from between two parked cars. Bundled up in a small pink anorak, she was looking lost and terribly frightened.

'What is it?' Taylor called, hurrying over to her, glad of the diversion from a conversation that could only have caused her more grief. Stooping down, she caught the child's sobbed, barely coherent response. It was obvious that the little girl had lost her mother.

'She can't be very far away,' Taylor gently reassured her, unprepared, as she stood up to look around for a likely candidate, for the tiny hand that instantly reached up to clasp hers.

How vulnerable they were, she agonised, assailed by a sudden deluge of emotions that were suffocating—almost overwhelming. And how trusting!

Tense lines scored her face and it was all she could do to keep it averted, not to let her feelings show as Jared joined them.

'What's all this? What's all the fuss about?' The tone he used with the child was gentle and consoling. Anguished, Taylor tried not to remember how much he had wanted children of his own.

A young woman, looking very fraught, was hurrying from the direction of the nearby Pay and Display machine.

'I told you not to run off!'

Reaching them, grabbing the errant child by the arm, she smiled apologetically at Taylor and Jared. But it was Jared for whom she spared a second glance before thanking them both profusely and pulling the now merely whimpering child back to her car.

'Are you all right?' Reaching Jared's saloon, Taylor could feel those shrewd eyes studying her across the gleaming black roof.

'Am *I* all right?' She still couldn't face him head on, risk his seeing the emotion that still misted her eyes. 'Why shouldn't I be?'

His mouth moved in a rather speculative way. 'You look…upset,' he remarked.

The car alarm system bleeped as he disengaged it. His eyes were still resting on her as he opened the driver's door.

'Why should I be upset? It's this infernal wind,' she prevaricated with her chin lifting in an unconscious gesture of defence against his probing. 'It's making my eyes water.'

Scepticism showed in the arching of an eyebrow, but Taylor was glad when he let it go at that.

What was he thinking? she wondered, sitting beside him in silence while he drove the short journey to her dentist. Was he wondering perhaps if she was remembering their marriage—her accidental and short, ill-fated pregnancy? If she was harbouring any regrets about losing her baby? Or even—from the cruel insinuations he had made at the time—any remorse?

Her chest ached from the misery of those memories, from recalling those bitter rows and the insecurities, brought on by the suspicions of his disloyalty, which vetoed any suggestion of their getting back together. Fortunately, however, he didn't seem to be pressing the point about trying again.

'I'll wait for you,' he said suddenly, bringing her back to the present with a jolt to realise that he was pulling up outside the dental practice.

'That won't be necessary,' she said in a flat voice, keen to get away from him. Seeing him again like this wasn't doing her any good at all. 'The station's just around the corner and it'll be easier and quicker for me to take the tube back to the studios.'

Fortunately he acknowledged this with a slight tilt of his head.

'In that case I'll call round next week.'

Why? she wanted to throw at him bitterly. *Why are you doing this to me?* But she held herself in check and was relieved at least to be able to tell him, 'You can't. I'm away on location next week.' The crew were filming a short documentary drama just outside of Edinburgh. 'After that I'm taking a week's leave.'

Jared switched off the engine as though he needed total silence to digest this information.

So that told you! Taylor thought, not caring if she had messed up his carefully calculated plans.

'Where are you going?'

She hadn't planned to go anywhere. She had been hoping

for a quiet time at home, baking, shopping and generally relaxing until her next pending assignment that promised to take her away again, abroad, for the best part of three weeks. But the last thing she wanted was to tell him that and so pulling a face she said, 'Who knows? I'm taking it as it comes. Right now I'm thinking it might be a good idea to stay in Scotland.'

'That's where you're filming, I take it?' It didn't require an answer. 'OK.' He exhaled heavily and, sounding suddenly bored, 'I'll see you when you get back. It's possible I'll be away myself the week after next. By the way, while you're up that way you could look into the Borrowdale house,' he went on to suggest rather wearily. 'I let it to the odd friend now and again but no one's using it at the moment. There are a few things of yours there, though—some you might consider to be of a sentimental nature. If you've no intention of going back there, you might prefer to have them with you,' he concluded, the cool delivery of his statement and his obvious acceptance that it was over between them sending a swift dart of pain down through her heart.

The house in Cumbria had been his late grandmother's and they had spent several long blissful weekends there between their return from Hawaii and that fateful party that had ruined all her illusions about her marriage.

'Give me a ring if you decide to...' with a hand as steady as his voice he was taking a card out of his wallet '...and I can arrange to have the place aired and heated for you.'

She looked at the small white card he handed her. As though she were one of his business associates, she thought achingly. It listed his office, email and fax numbers, which she already knew, plus the number of his new mobile phone.

'Thanks,' Taylor said, dropping it quickly into the open side compartment of her handbag because she would only have shown herself up by letting him see how much her own hands were shaking had she tried to undo the zip. 'If I decide to, I'll let you know.'

She was out of the car before he could detain her any longer but, as she turned towards the modern dental surgery, the sudden whirr of the passenger side window made her glance back.

'And Taylor!' He was leaning across the car's plush interior, his arm across the back of her vacated seat as she came back to see what it was he wanted. 'I just thought I ought to let you know. If you're planning to divorce me,' he said, 'then I think it only fair to tell you. I'll fight it every step of the way.'

The week's filming was over. Everything had gone smoothly and the crew were preparing to return to London.

Normally Taylor would have accompanied them in one of the company vehicles. She had, however, driven her own small hatchback to Scotland so that, with a week's leave ahead of her, she could make her way back to London at her own pace.

Now, watching Craig coiling up cables, and Paul loading lenses and other photographic equipment into the back of the wagon, reluctantly she considered Jared's suggestion about visiting Borrowdale while she was in the north.

It would probably be over a three-hour drive with the odd break, she calculated, depending on the road conditions, and the traffic, but that wasn't the reason why she wasn't keen to go. It was because the house held so many memories of a time when she had been so happy with Jared, and going there now would only emphasise how terribly wrong their marriage had gone; represent a finality she wasn't sure she could face. It would, however, be totally foolish not to go and collect her belongings from the house while she was up this way, she argued with herself. And wouldn't it be best to get things over and done with as soon as possible rather than prolong the inevitable?

'I'm glad at least that you've decided not to stay in Scotland,' Craig expressed when, having made up her mind, she told him of her plans. 'Some pretty heavy weather's forecast over the next few days. I'd come home as soon as you can.'

He himself couldn't wait to get back, Taylor realised fondly, if the number of times she had heard him ringing Charity over the past week was anything to go by.

'I will,' she promised, having not gone into too much depth about why she was stopping off in Cumbria. The truth of the situation hurt too much for her to share even with Craig.

The light was almost fading when she brought the car uphill from the bleak and lonely valley, and turned into the little lane where Jared's grandmother's house stood.

Snow had been threatening for most of the journey south and now the Lakeland sky above the glowering peaks of the mountains was an ominous purple.

Having been on the road since lunchtime, Taylor was happy to leave her car exactly where it was in the lane and brave the minus zero wind-chill factor to the house.

A three gabled, grey stone building with bay windows and a sloping drive, it stood alone above a rambling garden with spectacular views across the valley, and was, she remembered from those previous visits, large enough to feel spacious, while still managing to retain a cosy atmosphere.

She hadn't bothered telling Jared that she was coming. Speaking to him again would only have unsettled her, she had decided, and the task of clearing the house of her things was going to be painful enough without that. Besides, she still had a key.

Warmth was the first thing that struck her as soon as she

let herself in, which, though surprising, was more than welcome after the bitter, late Cumbrian afternoon.

Jared had obviously instructed someone to heat the place, she thought, probably guessing that if she did decide to follow his suggestion and turn up here, she would be too proud to ring him.

A small shiver ran through her as she considered just how well he knew her.

It was a relief to shed her thick grey overcoat and boots, and make herself a sandwich and a cup of tea with some of the basic provisions she had bought on the journey down. Only then, with the aid of sustenance, did she feel able to cope with the task ahead of her.

Everywhere she looked there were memories, but particularly in the country ambience of the sitting room with its comfortable sagging sofa and its rug-strewn, flagstone floor.

There were the pen and ink drawings she had sketched of the fells, on their first visit, and for which Jared had made rustic frames during their stay using his late-grandfather's tools, then hung them in the recesses either side of the huge stone fireplace. They belonged in this house. How could she take them down? Then there was the vast collection of books—mainly Jared's—on various shelves around the room—bursting with so many diverse subjects. Like travel and history, the Lakeland poets, psychology. Books on different cultures, religions and philosophies, all which reminded her of how well-read and well-travelled Jared was, of his staunch opinion that everyone had a voice, and deserved to be heard.

It was one of the reasons she had fallen in love with him, she remembered painfully, that depth of understanding and fairness he had always seemed to display towards most things, if not, in the end, towards her. And she had been overawed by his experience and his wealth of knowledge.

Having led what she considered to be a rather mundane

existence herself, his hard sophistication garnered from a shrewd determined brain and his twelve years seniority had excited her. How often had she lain on that old battered sofa with her head in his lap while he had talked about so many things and she had listened, rapt? And how willingly and wildly had she, on so many occasions afterwards, succumbed to that other kind of experience, the skilled mastery of his lovemaking?

How could things have gone so badly wrong? she wondered desolately, sliding her finger down the spine of a particularly large tome on world affairs. Because they had always made love. Even when they were breaking up they had still craved each other with a hunger that had bordered on desperation, the heat and bitterness of their rows somehow only seeming to kindle desire.

Perhaps if...

Her thoughts were brought up sharply by a sound outside in the hall. No, not in the hall, she thought. Outside the front door!

The wind was increasing in strength, playing with the metal disc over the keyhole. At least she tried reassuring herself that was all it was, until she realised the front door was being thrust forcibly open.

One of Jared's tenants!

Remembering he had said he sometimes let the place to friends, for a moment Taylor wondered if, as he hadn't heard from her, he had gone ahead and let someone else have the house this week. But no, he wouldn't do that, she thought, certain of it. Not when there was the slimmest chance of her coming here!

The door banged rather loudly, as though someone had kicked it closed, and quickly, snatching up the brass poker from the hearth, Taylor raced out into the hall.

'Are you going to hit me with that?' Stopping dead, Jared was grimacing down at the potential weapon Taylor was holding. 'Or is this some new type of fell-walking aid?' He was carrying two bags of groceries, balancing one on each arm, and sleet was glistening on his jet-black hair.

'It's you.' Heart still thumping, Taylor's shoulders sagged with relief.

'I'm sorry.' Casually dressed in dark trousers and a black anorak, he was shouldering his way past her. 'I didn't mean to alarm you.'

Didn't mean...? Flabbergasted, Taylor demanded, 'What are you doing here?'

Ignoring her question, he carried the bags into the square, old-fashioned kitchen, dumped them down on the table and started to unpack them.

'What are you doing?' Taylor breathed, following, not frightened or shocked any more, just angry. 'Why are you here?'

'I spent an awful lot of my childhood in this house,' he told her. 'I also happen to own it.' His long hands were dealing with tins and cartons and packages. 'I think that gives me the right to come here whenever I get the chance.'

'Not while I'm here,' she returned uncompromisingly. Standing in her thin socks, she could feel the cold striking up from the hard stone floor.

'Really?' For a moment he stopped what he was doing, while his gaze moved over her jean and sweater-clad slenderness with disconcerting intensity. 'I can't think of a better reason to come.'

'Jared!' How could he do this to her? A justifiable hurt anger lined her fine features and with it increasing puzzlement. 'You said you'd be away...' She remembered him saying that in the car when he had dropped her outside the dental surgery.

'I am away,' he said calmly. 'And put down that poker. You're making me feel at a distinct disadvantage.'

Him—at a disadvantage! 'You lied to me,' she accused, ignoring him.

'No I didn't.'

'Tricked me then.' Tensely her fingers tightened on the cold brass rod. 'Why didn't you tell me?'

'Because, one,' he said, as though he needed to emphasise his point, 'I wasn't sure whether I'd be able to get here or not. And two, if I had said I was coming, you wouldn't have.'

Resentfully she watched him moving around the kitchen, unable to drag her reluctant gaze from his long lean frame as he reached up to open a wall cupboard. 'Whatever gave you that idea?'

'And put on some shoes or slippers before you catch your death of cold,' he advised without looking at her, taking no heed of her little burst of sarcasm.

She stayed right where she was, however, even though her feet were freezing, simply because he had instructed otherwise. 'Don't change the subject.'

'All right. I wanted to be with you. Is that direct enough for you?'

He turned to face her, his eyes glittering with a cold and feral anger.

For a moment his declaration seemed to tear the breath out of her lungs, as powerfully as the wind was tearing at the eaves and chimneys of the old house.

'Why?' she said at length, struggling for composure under the influence of his formidable masculinity. 'So you can take advantage of my weakness and failure ever to resist you?'

The carrier bags rustled as he screwed them up, opened a drawer and stuffed them inside. He sent a wry, sidelong glance down over his shoulder. 'Not while you're holding that poker.'

She slung it down, making a point, drawing herself up to her full height. 'I'm not afraid of you.'

'Good!' He thrust the drawer closed, swung away from it. 'Because I'm sure as hell afraid of you!'

Taylor eyed him with some surprise, a pained query darkening her eyes. 'Am I so much of a harridan?'

'A harridan?' Coming back across the kitchen, he laughed rather harshly. 'God! I wish you were. At least I'd know how to deal with that. It wouldn't be any hardship to me to tame a shrew.'

She shuddered, thinking how lethal his brand of taming might be. What woman would stand a chance against his dark and dangerous sensuality? She might feign to put up a fight against it for a while but, in the end, all but the most indifferent would succumb.

'Oh, no.' His breath seemed to shiver through him as he stood there now, contemplating, regarding her. 'You're quite the opposite, Taylor. Reticent. Uncommunicative. Almost frighteningly aloof. Like a deep, mysterious lake. I used to think it was an admirable quality. In fact, my dear, I must confess, it turned me on—like hell! But there's a limit to how much unmelted butter a man can get through, even if it's the loveliest mouth he's being tempted by. Tell me, Taylor, are you really as cold as you seem? Or is there a real warm woman in there somewhere trying desperately hard to get out? Begging to be rescued from her own worst enemy—herself!'

Is that how he saw her? As a cold, unfeeling human being? With a heart of ice, as other men had accused her of having? Was that why he had been so ready to believe she could hurt her unborn child? Care for nothing but herself? Her independence? Her job?

Pain clouded her eyes and swiftly her lashes came down to hide it. 'And you think one night trapping me here with you,' she uttered, cultivating even more of the apparent coolness he had ridiculed, 'will loosen all my inhibitions—bring out the real warm woman—' her tone was bitterly emphatic '—you seem so sure is there?'

'Believe me, a man would have to be a genius and it would take more than one night and a diamond cutter to chip through that glacial shell of yours, Taylor. If it is a shell. And I'm hardly trapping you,' he reminded her brusquely before she could say anything. 'You came voluntarily.'

'And I'll be leaving voluntarily. First thing in the morning!' she retorted, swinging away.

'Of course.' She heard a cupboard being opened, heard it bang forcefully closed again. 'I've got to hand it to you, Taylor. You're beautiful. Talented. Self-sufficient. But where relationships are concerned, it's what you do best, isn't it?'

'What?' she queried pointedly. Her eyes were dark and questioning as she turned around.

'Running away.'

Because she had done exactly that. *You'll run away.* Because it was inherent in her. *You'll always run away.*

Her breath catching in her throat, she brought her cupped hands up to her nose and mouth, her eyes closing for a few moments while she steeled herself against retaliating.

'Are you all right?'

He'd asked her that in the car park, she remembered, last Friday after that tense, disconcerting lunch she had shared with him.

He was standing right next to her now. Her body was absorbing his dangerous warmth like a soothing balm through her skin and his scent impinged on her nostrils like an intoxicating musk.

'Taylor?'

When his fingers touched her arm, however, panicking she jerked away.

'Of course I am! Why shouldn't I be?' she protested and, for the sake of her cold feet and her equilibrium, moved away from him, towards the hall.

He had discarded his anorak when he joined her in the sitting room and the thick black casual shirt he was wearing with his dark trousers was unbuttoned at the throat.

Standing, sorting through some books, Taylor glanced up, her senses leaping as her interest fell too willingly on the hint of crisp dark body hair peeping out over the top of his shirt, emphasising the corded strength of his throat.

'I see you've eaten.' His gaze was resting on the mug and the plate, which contained the remains of her sandwich. 'Or put up some show of eating.'

Taylor snapped closed the poetry book she had been looking at. A book of love poems. A book he had bought for her to celebrate their being married for two weeks.

There was dark emotion behind the challenge in the green eyes that clashed with his. 'Did you come here to start criticising my diet?'

'No.' His mouth tugged down on one side. 'But it's a darned good idea. Somebody needs to.'

'Why? Worried about me?' A little hint of sarcasm slipped out, unheeded, unchecked.

'Of course.'

'Well, don't be. I can take care of myself.'

'Can you?' His gaze was tugging over the creamy polo-necked sweater she had been wearing when he had first turned up at Charity's over a week ago, moving down over her small breasts and waistline and the barest suggestion of curved hips beneath her fitted jeans. 'You could have fooled me.'

Why? she wanted to throw at him. *Because I haven't been able to eat properly since I saw you again? Because I can't get you out of my mind and because when you're around you dominate everything I think, say and do?*

Instead, taking another book out of the bookcase, turning it over in her hands, she said, 'When did you get here anyway?'

He slipped his hands into his pockets. 'This afternoon. I switched on the heating and went into town to stock up on some things while the house was warming up,' he told her.

Broodingly she watched him cross the room, pick up the plate and the used mug she had left on the side of the hearth.

'This place always did bring out the best in you, didn't it, Taylor?' He gestured with the mug he was dangling from one finger, his mouth moving wryly. 'Back in London this would have been in the dishwasher before it was even cold.'

She looked up from the book she was making a performance of studying. 'Meaning?'

'Your penchant for order is commendable but sometimes it can be bloody infuriating. It would do you good to be slovenly occasionally. Mess up your hair. Rough it for a while.'

She gritted her teeth against what she considered was yet another of his totally unjust analyses of her.

'Don't you have business to attend to?' Pushing back a strand of the expertly cut hair to which he had metaphorically referred, she watched him move over to the door. 'Something important you've left that can't possibly proceed without you being around?' It was one of the reasons for their arguments, she remembered; his always having to work late—something that hadn't helped lessen her suspicions about him having an affair—and his going away so much, especially when he'd had the gall to accuse *her* of only being interested in her career!

'No.' He sounded remarkably decisive. 'I meant it when I said that I think we should get back together. When two people have what we had, I think it's no less than stupidity to throw it all away.'

'What you had you mean,' she said softly, hurting. Hadn't he had a mistress—and the luxury of a convenient wife?

He moved back into the room, setting the mug and plate down on the low table that filled the space on the rug between the long comfortable sofa and a deeply cushioned chair.

'Are you saying you didn't get anything out of it too? Because, my pretty wife, it wouldn't be too much punishment to me to have to remind you.'

'No!' She took a step back, seeing the steely resolve burning in his eyes, relaxing a little when he stopped, clearly thinking twice about carrying out his threat.

'I thought you'd accepted my decision,' she expressed, uncomfortably conscious of the tremor in her voice. 'I thought that was the reason why I'm here...' a toss of her chin indicated the books she was holding '...doing all this.' Puzzled green eyes searched those that were as dark and impenetrable as midnight. 'It was the last thing you said—about me not divorcing you...'

His black brows came together while he inclined his head in the way he always did when something puzzled him, a gesture that was so poignantly familiar to her that she found herself battling with a host of treacherous emotions.

'I said that there were things of yours here that you might want to have with you. Things I thought you might be missing or might even have forgotten you had. It wasn't my intention for you to start clearing them out. You accused me of assuming too much, Taylor. Well I'm not the only one who's been guilty of that. And what I said was, that if you tried to divorce me, I'd fight it all the way, and I will—until you come to your senses and realise that it was only your petty jealousies and suspicions that broke us up in the first place.'

How could he say that?

Taylor gritted her teeth, decided not to challenge that statement. Instead she said in a much steadier voice, 'So I just jump back into your bed and everything will be all right?'

A nerve tugged in his jaw for a few silent seconds, the only life in a face that might have been chiselled out of rock.

'If that's all I thought it would take, we wouldn't be standing here now,' he answered her softly, his arrogance, with what his words conjured up, sending a menacing excitement licking through her veins.

He knew her intimately; from every small fantasy to every last sensitive part of her body, and he had recognised that dangerous attraction that still existed between them. OK. Perhaps he hadn't come here to capitalise on it, she accepted, but he knew, as well as she did, that if he tried to seduce her back into his bed, she wouldn't stand a chance against his lethal skill and charisma. And if she stayed here, who knew what sort of fool she could wind up making of herself over him—and at what cost to her self-respect?

Pain warred with anger over his audacity and the knowledge that he had, indeed, tricked her. Without a thought for what she wanted. Without a care about how it might affect her in the end!

'I'm sorry for misconstruing all your motives,' she uttered tightly. 'But there's one thing I'm not leaving either of us under any misconceptions about.' Nimbly she stooped to scoop up the plate and mug he had put down on the table. 'I'm still leaving here first thing tomorrow morning.'

CHAPTER FOUR

IT WAS the silence that woke her. The thick, heavy silence and the light that burned with a peculiar brightness through the chintzy curtains.

Snug in the small double bed in the smaller of the two main bedrooms she had opted to sleep in the previous night, Taylor was reluctant for a moment to give up its warmth.

Suddenly though, as realisation dawned, she was pushing back the duvet and racing over to the window, gasping as she pulled back the curtains.

Everything was white—the garden, the trees and the hill-sides, dazzling—like the mountains beyond them—under a crisp heavy fall of virgin snow.

She shivered, wondering why the air felt so icy, and went over to feel the radiator on the opposite wall. It was stone cold.

Fetching her light robe from the bathroom, quickly she slipped it on, pushing her hair into place with agitated fingers.

Jared must have gone to bed without setting the heating to come on, or the thermostat in the hall was too low, she thought, racing downstairs to set the control higher. Either that, or it had come on and gone off again hours ago which meant that Jared wasn't even up yet. Which was unlike him, she remembered from their marriage, when he had been up at six most days of the week.

As she reached the hall, sounds coming from the sitting room brought her up sharply.

Jared?

She could smell smoke now—wood smoke—and could

hear what she instantly distinguished as the crackling of an open fire.

He didn't see her at first. He had his back to the door and was bending over the fireplace, tossing logs from a wicker basket onto the brightly burning flames, and the sight of him performing that simple, domestic chore tugged unexpectedly at something deep down inside Taylor.

Greedy for the smallest chance to feast her eyes on him, undetected, her hungry gaze tugged unashamedly over his pleasing torso.

He was wearing a dark-blue cable-knit sweater and jeans, which showed off the superbly fit lines of his body. His hair was waving, dark and thick, over the polo neck of his sweater, while the thick wool encased shoulders that could set themselves squarely against anything that promised trouble. His hips were hard and lean, his buttocks tightly muscled, and even through the denim his long legs looked packed with the whipcord strength of a hunter. On his feet he wore a pair of casual black shoes, but it was his hands to which Taylor's eyes were ultimately drawn; those long sinewy hands that could apply themselves to any manual task, however mundane, seeing it through with the same skilled competence with which they could also caress and arouse a woman...

'So you're up.'

He turned round so suddenly that he couldn't have failed to notice her interest in him and, from the rather sensual amusement tugging at his mouth it was clear he hadn't.

'You should have woken me,' she protested, blushing and tousled in her dressing gown and slippers. She had slept for hours, she realised, having claimed a headache and gone to bed straight after their light dinner last night.

'Why? Are you going somewhere?' He was grinning so shamelessly that she wanted to hit him.

With an exasperated glance at him, she hurried over to

the window. Unlike her bedroom, the sitting room faced the lane and she could just make out her car, virtually buried beneath a thick mound of snow.

'Still thinking of leaving, Taylor?' The deep tones were overlaid with mockery, and she whipped round, eyes daring him to carry his joking any further. It didn't help having noticed that he had had the foresight to put his own car straight in the garage when he had driven in last night.

'I suppose you think this is all very funny!' She moved away from the window, rubbing her arms, shoulders hunched against the cold.

'Are you going to blame me for this too?'

No, of course she wasn't. It was his complacency she couldn't take, which made her reply in a way that sounded childish even to her own ears, 'You knew I was bent on leaving here this morning.'

'Then start walking.' Suddenly he wasn't amused any more. The alarmingly swift movement that brought him to face her had her recoiling from him. His teeth were clenched between grim lips and his whole face was harsh with anger. Lifting her chin, Taylor caught the strong scent of wood smoke clinging to his sweater, with the underlying freshness of the great outdoors. 'I've got enough problems here without you whingeing and whining like some petulant little schoolgirl.' He swung back to resume tending to the fire. 'I can't help the damned weather, all right! Contrary to what you think I didn't order it to help me with some Machiavellian scheme to trap someone who's made it very plain she clearly doesn't want to be married to me—because if you're going to be like this for the next two or three days, believe me, it's not going to be any picnic for me either!'

Two or three days? Mentally Taylor shook that unsettling possibility aside, aware of Jared's anger in every movement of his body, the way he was suddenly tossing logs onto the fire with more vehemence than before, sending sparks and ash flying up into the huge chimney. She supposed she deserved his anger, in a way.

'Problems?' she repeated tentatively to his broad back, wanting to smooth things over between them. 'What problems? What's happened?'

He stood up again, one hand on the back pocket of his jeans. A deep sigh lifted the thick cable stitch of his sweater. 'The snow's brought the power cables down. There's no electricity. No heating. That means no hot food or water—except in any way we can improvise ourselves.'

A barely audible, shocked little oath escaped her.

'Exactly,' he said. 'So you see, I didn't instigate the weather or this situation. Nor do I like it, though I will reiterate what I said last night. I wanted some time with you.'

'Why?'

'To sort out our differences.'

'You think they can be sorted out?'

'I don't know, but I sure as hell want to try. I'm not proud of having the label of *Failed Marriage* stamped on my head either. Isn't that why you kept your marital status a secret from Charity and Craig?'

Taylor's back stiffened. How well he knew her! Or was it simply from the realms of his knowledge marked *Human Psychology*, gleaned from life and the wealth of books he kept in his own extensive library?

'I saw coming here as an opportunity, that's all. An opportunity for us to talk—relax—without the pressures of our jobs, life or anything else getting in the way.'

She let out a short brittle laugh because he had given her no say in the matter. Apart from which they had tried before; tried and failed, and it had only resulted in pain, pain that, even until he had stormed into her life again, hadn't even really begun to ease.

'And supposing I don't go along with your optimism—don't share your idealistic view of what you think our marriage should be? Don't want to be here?'

A hint of a smile touched his mouth as he looked from her flushed and finely contoured face towards the window and the heavy snowfall that imprisoned them.

'I hate to say this, darling, but I hardly think you have a choice.'

He was chopping logs when she came back downstairs, having already cleared the path at the back of the house leading from the kitchen to the log store.

He was wearing black rubber boots now, pulled high and tightly over his jeans. His black hair was falling forward as he worked. Wielding the axe against the backdrop of the snow-swept valley and the awesome vastness of the sparkling mountains, he looked like the wild man of the moor, Taylor fancied, feeling the tug of something reckless inside of her as she stepped out into the biting air.

Throwing down the axe, he glanced up and saw her.

'That's much more practical,' he commented laconically with a swift appraisal of her thick dark sweater, warm trousers and sensible shoes before bending again to his task.

He was using a large steel wedge to split the logs he had already chopped, driving it into the wood with a mallet, the strike of metal on metal ringing out across the frozen hillside.

He was working hard—looked hot, Taylor thought, volunteering, 'Do you want any help?'

He paused from his work, one booted foot resting on the cut ring of a tree trunk he was using as a platform to split the logs, a hand resting on a denim-clad knee.

'Are you any good with an axe?'

She looked at him uncertainly, then at the implement lying beside him.

Well, she had never done it before, but there was always a first time, she thought, moving to pick it up.

'Don't be silly,' he said, so that she realised then that he was joking. 'Go and see if you can rustle up something appetising for breakfast. Bacon, scrambled eggs and blueberry pancakes will do to start.'

'Ha!' Her laugh rose on a cloud of warm vapour before she glanced back at him over her shoulder. 'You wish,' she told him with a grimace, going back along the cleared path and wondering how she was even going to heat any water let alone anything else.

As it turned out, she found the answer almost immediately in the large black kettle, only kept now for ornamental purposes on the hearth. She supposed it had been used domestically in Jared's grandmother's day, in the larger fireplace in the kitchen that now housed the modern equivalent of the old range. Even that needed electricity to operate it, she thought rather despairingly, pulling a face as she picked up the ancient kettle.

Gratefully, however, she took it out into the kitchen, half filled it, then struggled with it into the sitting room, first adding more logs to the fire to make a flat surface for the kettle to stand on, before placing it carefully on top. Only then did she decide it was safe to leave, before grabbing the pale fleece she had unpacked and hung in the hall the previous night and venturing back outside.

'What will we do if the pipes freeze?' she called out worriedly to Jared, coming down the path to where he was filling the wicker basket with logs. 'If we can't get any water?' While filling the kettle it had suddenly struck her how much worse things could get.

'Don't worry,' he said, seeing her concern. 'There's next to no chance of that happening. With these Lakeland winters no one risks being without the necessary insulation. They're far more diligent about such things up here than we are in the south. The place was already well protected when my grandmother was alive but then just before she died I persuaded her to let me get a major reinsulating job done. Grandmother was stubborn—fiercely independent and quite unmovable in most things—but I was determined she'd let me do that much, though I must admit, she did put up quite a fight.'

Taylor smiled, catching the fond note in his voice, regretting that she had never met the kind-looking grey-haired woman who had died the year before she had met Jared and whose photograph stood in a little silver frame on the tall oak chest in the room she was occupying. It was taken with Jared's grandfather, almost on the spot where Taylor was standing. She had a feeling that it was Jared who had taken it.

'You loved her a lot, didn't you?' she remarked, slipping her hands into the pockets of her fleece to keep them warm. His grandfather too, she thought, remembering how he had said that when his own father had died just before his second birthday, his grandparents had opted to look after him when their daughter-in-law had insisted on pursuing her acting career.

For an answer he simply went on tossing logs into the basket.

'Were you close to your mother?' It surprised her to realise that, despite having lived with him for more than eighteen months, there was still a lot about him she had failed to discover.

'Not as close as I would have liked.'

'Did she visit very often?'

'No.' The log he threw made a dull 'chick' as it landed on top of the others, alarming a little brown dunnock that had been foraging around with scant hope of finding a staple meal of insects, worms or seeds beneath the heavy covering of snow. Watching it hop unobtrusively beneath a winter jasmine which was bravely sporting its bright yellow flowers against the boundary wall, Taylor made a mental note to put down some scraps. 'She didn't like Cumbria,' Jared was enlarging then. 'She liked bright lights and city life.'

'Does she still live in New York?'

He stopped what he was doing, and stood, stern-mouthed, looking out across the snow-laden hedge to the silent valley.

'No,' he said at length. 'She died. A couple of months ago.'

'She...' Taylor stared at his dark, tousled hair as he stooped to finish loading the last few logs into the basket. 'How?' she whispered, shocked.

'She had a crippling illness that came on gradually over the past fifteen months or so,' he surprised her by saying. 'I spent a lot of time going backwards and forwards to the States. If I hadn't, I would have come looking for you a long time ago,' he interjected grimly, without looking at her, which explained why she hadn't seen or heard from him for so long, Taylor realised, her heart going out to him over what must have been an extremely difficult time. 'I tried to spend as much time with her as I could during her last months and I suppose we became closer than we had ever been throughout our lives. After all, she did her best for me—gave me everything,' he said, with something of the strain he must have suffered showing briefly in that hard, handsome face. 'But I would have traded it all for some of her time.'

'Why didn't you tell me?' Taylor whispered, catching that note of deep regret—the loss—for what might have been—in that last, softly uttered statement.

She had only met the woman once. It was shortly after their wedding when they had come back from Hawaii. A fading actress who had never really achieved star status,

Calista Steele had been in London with an equally fading male counterpart and had called to see them at Jared's penthouse flat.

Tall and elegant, with a swathe of grey streaking her thick black hair, the woman had nevertheless possessed the same awesome detachment as her son. And while there had seemed to be a deep respect for each other, between mother and son, Taylor had noticed no real display of obvious affection in their relationship.

'Why didn't you let me know?' she repeated emphatically.

'When?' His voice, as he swung the basket up into his arms, was harshly cynical. 'Yesterday? Last week? Or at the time?'

'Well…' Taylor gave a quick bewildered shake of her head. She couldn't believe something like that could have happened to him and she hadn't even known about it. 'At the time of course.'

'I didn't feel I needed to involve you when you'd made it quite plain you no longer wanted any part in my life— even if I had known where you were.' He was all muscle and fitness striding ahead of her down the path, those brawny shoulders effectively blocking her out.

'You thought I wouldn't care because I couldn't live up to what you wanted me to be?'

'And what was that?' he threw back over his shoulder.

'A dutiful wife and mother.' She hadn't intended to get back on this subject but his low opinion of her hurt more than she could have imagined possible. 'Ready to turn a blind eye to any other woman you wanted in your life. Effectively second best!'

He stopped, turning so abruptly that she almost collided with the wicker basket. The cold anger in his eyes chilled her more than the bitterly cold day.

'Is that what you thought you were?'

'Wasn't I?'

'What you thought I wanted? An obedient little mouse and bed partner? Someone I could manipulate and bend easily to my will? What respect do you think I would have had for you—for myself—if I'd thought that was all you—and I—were worthy of? Credit me with some ethics, Taylor, because we did have *something*, only you were too damn blinkered to see it!'

Feeling unjustly chastened, she retorted heatedly, 'Too besotted, you mean, not to see what was going on!'

'What was going on, dearest, was all inside your head. Oh, I admit Alicia tried to ring me a few times, but that didn't mean I was still seeing her. As I told you before, it was your petty jealousies and suspicions that killed our marriage—nothing else!'

'That isn't true!'

'Isn't it?'

Those inky eyes seemed to be penetrating right through to her soul and his features were as bleak suddenly as the ice-packed fells across the valley.

Of course, he was probably still mourning his mother, Taylor thought, chastising herself for not having immediately realised that. Regrettably she wished she had kept her mouth shut.

'Believe it if you want to,' she said wearily, tired of continually fighting with him. She was relieved when he turned and carried on down the path.

With her eyes on his broad back she considered what he had said about her doubts and suspicions all being in her head. Were they? she wondered wretchedly. Certainly he had done nothing to allay her fears and insecurities. So what was he saying? That it had all been her fault? Their rows? Her refusal even to entertain having his children?

When he had been flaying her with his hurtful insinuations about terminating their unborn child—accusing her of wanting nothing but her precious job, had he, she wondered suddenly, somehow been comparing her with his mother?

'Come inside,' he commanded gently, as though sensitive to her change of mood and, with unerring courtesy, stood aside to let her pass.

The kettle was singing on the fire as they came back inside the house. The sound was comforting, helping to lift Taylor's downcast spirits.

'I'm afraid I can't conjure up anything more than plain bread and rock-hard butter,' she murmured, hearing him come into the kitchen just as she was lifting the lid off the butter dish. At least they had plenty of the basic foods, she thought with some sense of relief, since Jared had doubled up on some of the provisions she had brought last night.

'Is that so,' he said, not sounding at all perturbed. 'Then you go and make the tea—' he was thrusting a teapot into her hands '—and I'll see to whatever has to be done here.'

Taylor was only too glad to. Standing in a cold kitchen, making holes in fresh bread with unspreadable butter wasn't her idea of fun, she thought, adding cups, saucers and a jug of milk to a tray with the teapot, before carrying them through into the welcoming warmth of the sitting room.

She had just made the tea and was sitting on the rug in front of the fire when he strode in carrying another tray.

'Crumpets!' she breathed delightedly, her face aglow as he set them down on the low table she had dragged nearer the fire. They looked plump and soft. Hungrily she watched him spear one with a toasting fork.

'Always look further than only at what at first appears to be apparent,' he advised, and she knew he wasn't just talking about the crumpets. 'We used to do this on winter nights just for the sheer hell of it.'

We. 'You and your grandparents,' Taylor supplied, surprised that he had never confided even that small piece of information to her before.

His mouth compressed in wry contemplation as he stood there, turning the fork expertly before the flame. The crumpet was beginning to brown and it smelled yeasty and delicious as it cooked. 'They were good days. Especially when my grandfather was alive.'

'They must have been.' Taylor sat back from pouring tea into the two cups she had set down on the hearth, drawing her legs up under her. It was easy to visualise how things must have been, the domestic, happy family scene. It was something she had not known. Not in the same secure, taken-for-granted way...

'Ouch!' he said, shaking his hand, bringing her attention to the fact that, in turning the crumpet, Jared had just burnt his finger.

'Hot?' she taunted laughingly.

'Not so you'd notice.'

She looked up into his strong abstracted features, flushed from the heat of the fire. He hadn't shaved, either because of an uncharged razor or because he had had more important things to do. But in his country clothes, with that dark stubble shading his jaw, he looked at ease, relaxed and totally at home.

Often, in his high-powered world, sporting his clean-cut executive image she had tried to imagine him as a child and hadn't been able to. Now, away from the pressures of the fast lane in which he functioned, here amidst the rugged country where he seemed to belong, she could see him as a gangling youth, obstinate, determined, a free spirit. She could visualize him sitting here with his grandparents on winter nights, and, during the summer, fishing for minnows in the tumbling becks, running barefoot, wild as the moorland and the fells.

Her eyes still trained on his formidably handsome features, almost involuntarily Taylor murmured, 'This place brings out the best in you, too.'

His cruel mouth slackened broodingly as he gazed down on her, those black eyes holding hers with such dark power that she couldn't look away. Sitting there on the rug she felt like a slender flower beneath the shadow of a great tree whose daunting presence was capable of blocking out the sunlight from her life, or giving her the strength to grow and thrive from its protection.

With their eyes linked, Taylor felt the stark desire that seemed to flow from the very root of him, filling her with a mutual need that rose like a dark and dangerous sap through her veins. Her breath came shallowly as her pulse rate quickened, and her throat ached so that she had to swallow to ease its dryness.

Light flared in his face at the same instant as Taylor smelled the smoke, became aware that the crumpet he was toasting had caught fire.

'Look what you're doing!' she gasped with a shaky little laugh, catching the oath he uttered before he swiftly pushed the charcoaled offering, still flaming, onto a plate.

'You'll never make Chef of the Year like this!' she laughed, more easily now, relieved that the emotion-charged moment was past.

'Perhaps Chef of the Year doesn't have the world's sexiest siren to distract him,' he chastised, defending himself as he speared another crumpet with the fork.

Putting a lump of butter on the blackened pikelet, careful not to burn her hands, Taylor watched the gold butter melt instantly across its surface, filling the holes. The way he could melt her resistance—fill her—she thought shamefully, and didn't say anything because it was safer that way.

Breakfast was delicious, she decided, watching Jared chomp his way through at least a plateful of his own efforts, while Taylor surprised herself by eating at least three of the crumpets. She had brought some honey with her from Edinburgh and while Jared had refused it, she had indulged herself, spreading it thickly over each warm buttered mound.

'That's better,' Jared commented when she put her plate down on the hearth, having finished every last crumb. 'That's the most I've seen you eat since we've been together.'

Lounging beside him on the rug, Taylor tensed.

'We aren't back together,' she reminded him swiftly. She had made no such agreement, nor was she ready to.

'Of course not.' He flashed her a smile that didn't quite warm his eyes. 'I was speaking figuratively.'

She shrugged. 'Well, don't presume, Jared. I haven't said I'm coming back to you.'

'Taylor,' he exhaled, the way he addressed her alone assuring her he wasn't exactly very pleased. 'The last thing I would ever do with you is presume.'

Feeling strangely chastised, Taylor looked down at her greasy fingers. A small trail of honey clung to the third finger of her left hand, she noticed, with her little finger splayed.

'No,' she uttered, her breath coming rapidly when Jared grabbed her hand and she saw the purpose in his face, realised his intention.

'Stop me,' he whispered, and it was a deeply sensual challenge.

CHAPTER FIVE

LIKE a rabbit mesmerised by a fox, Taylor watched him watching her even as he dipped his head and his mouth closed over her honeyed finger.

There was desire in his eyes, more potent and deadly than that which she had seen burning in them earlier.

'Jared...' She closed her eyes against the raw need she saw in him, against the ache of a new kind of hunger in herself that only this man could assuage. The suckling warmth of his mouth brought with it images of the pleasurable nights she had shared in his bed, the provocative action of his tongue encircling her finger calling forth more erotic imagery, of pleasing him, of his pleasuring her in the most intimate and earth-shattering ways so that remembering produced a deep sensual throb in her lower body.

She opened her eyes. He was still watching her, his proud dark face flushed now from more than the heat of the fire.

'You used to taste like this all over. Remember, Taylor? You gave me honey every time I took you to bed. Like a queen bee paralysing me with her sweetness until I could do nothing but surrender to your hold over me—and still I could never get enough of you.'

His voice trembled with the depth of his desire. If he had been trying to turn her on, he had succeeded, but only at the expense of his own self-possession. Without even looking at him she could tell he was aroused, and she found herself craving the demands of his rock-hard body. He would be big and ready to take her. Helplessly, she realised, she wanted him to do just that. Push her back against the rug and come down heavily on top of her, give her no choice but to submit to him so that she could drown in the ecstasy of his driving passion, sate this unbelievable need of him and not feel afterwards that she had relinquished her pride or determination to be free.

With every gram of her will, she dragged herself back from the brink of stupidity to say shakily, 'But you didn't love me.'

For a moment his fingers tightened around her slim hand.

'Didn't I?' His lips had moved to play erotically over the perfumed flesh of her wrist, and yet the eyes that continued to hold hers were intensely probing, assessing, and as unfathomable as the darkest night.

'Let me go.'

Surprisingly, he complied at once.

'I'd better get some more logs in,' he said heavily, getting to his feet, as though he were totally unaffected by what had just happened between them.

But he had been. And severely, Taylor thought, watching him scoop up the wicker basket and carry it back across the room.

Even so, it felt like another put-down. Like he had been testing her, she decided bitterly, her spirits lowering like the sudden drop in the room temperature as he went through the kitchen and opened the back door, letting in the biting air from outside.

They spent the rest of the day treading carefully around each other, treating each other with polite caution as though each was reluctant to delve too deeply into what the other might be thinking or feeling.

The first thing they did after Taylor had found enough scraps to feed the birds was to search the house for candles, finding the half-burned remains of one, still in its holder, in the cupboard under the kitchen sink.

'That isn't going to last an evening!' Taylor groaned de-

spairingly, then found a whole boxful while she was looking in the electricity meter cupboard under the stairs.

'So you won't have to worry about being left in the dark
with me after all,' Jared commented dryly when she rushed
eagerly back to the kitchen to acquaint him with her find.

Taylor didn't respond, sensing that there was more than
one meaning behind that outwardly innocuous remark but,
apart from that, the day continued on an otherwise even
course.

Wrapped up in warm layers, scarves and gloves, together
they scraped the snow from the drive that sloped upwards
alongside the house, making a clear path to the lane. Then
Taylor beat the soft snow from the bonnet and roof of her
car, opened the electrically operated door to the adjoining
garage that was a later addition to the house, and climbed
into her car with the intention of putting it away.

Unfortunately the little hatchback refused to comply immediately; coughing and spluttering each time she turned
the ignition key.

'Problems?'

Jared was beside her open door, big and capable, ready
to lend a hand.

'It's just cold,' she said, silently urging it to start, which,
fortunately, it did after a bit of gentle coaxing with the
ignition.

'The drive's treacherous. I'd leave it right where it is,'
he advised grimly.

'No, I'd prefer to put it away.' She didn't like the thought
of her car—her key to self-sufficiency—being left out in
such extreme conditions.

'Then perhaps you'd better let me do it,' he suggested,
looking every bit like taking over. 'I intended to put it away
last night but I'm afraid seeing you swept all my good
intentions out of the window.'

'I can manage,' Taylor assured him firmly, deciding to

ignore his comment as she pulled the door closed, shutting him out.

If he could do it, why couldn't she? she thought, conscientiously steering the car towards the open garage.

Having never negotiated the drive before, however, she hadn't reckoned on the unexpected swing to the left at the top of the incline, or the sheet of ice just outside the garage door.

Pressing her foot down on the accelerator, needing a few more revs to accommodate the slope, she had almost levelled up when the back wheels started to spin alarmingly.

Feeling the car starting to slide, she braked instinctively, but too hard, she realised too late, and with a sinking heart felt the back wheels pull away from her as the car skidded with an ominous scraping into the steel frame of the garage door.

'Oh…!' She swallowed the small invective, uncertain as to what hurt most as Jared rushed up to survey the damage, her loss of face or what she might have done to her car.

'I'm afraid you've put a hell of a crease in the front wing,' he called over his shoulder before moving back to open her door. 'Good try,' he breathed in a way that left her unsure as to whether he was praising her efforts or being sarcastic. 'But you'd better let me take it from here.'

This time Taylor didn't argue. If she had she could only have wound up making an even bigger fool of herself, she decided, and she was feeling bad enough as it was.

With banked resentment that she knew was totally unjustified, she watched him put the car into reverse gear, pull back and set it easily on a straight course into the garage, bringing it to a halt beside the dark gleaming lines of his own saloon.

Shoulders hunched, she was waiting on the drive as he used the remote control switch to close the garage doors—a feature that certainly hadn't been there in his grandmother's time, she was certain—and as he strode back down to her she gripped her upper arms as though to fend off more than the freezing air.

'There you are. All safe and sound where nothing can touch it,' he said dryly and now she knew he was mocking her. 'Does it hurt so much to let me help you?' he enquired, walking beside her back down the drive. She wasn't looking at him but she could feel his eyes resting on her with a regard that was as ruthless and penetrating as the icy wind. 'Is it just me you want to prove your independence to? Or are you the same with every other man?'

'So I pranged my car.' The sparkling hillsides were almost painful to her eyes and she dragged her dazzled gaze away, tossing over her shoulder, 'Do you have to make such an issue of it?'

There was a side gate in the low hedge that separated the drive from the garden. He reached around her, opening it with a sharp click of the latch.

'One day, Taylor, you might realise—to use an old cliché...' he held the gate open as she preceded him through '...that no man—or woman—is an island. We all need each other.'

She didn't answer, mainly because passing so close to him she was all too aware of his long, lean body—of his dark and dangerous persona—dangerous to her at any rate, she decided, sticking out her chin, fighting against the truth of his words.

Perhaps he was right, she thought, hearing the gate close behind them. But needing someone too much left you exposed and vulnerable, didn't it? Hadn't she learnt that lesson long ago, with the bitter betrayal of that first and fundamental trust?

They had sandwiches for lunch with the tinned salmon Jared had bought in town, then they boiled more water to wash up and were glad to get back into the warm sitting room where Jared heaped more wood on to the fire, and where, for the rest of the afternoon, they talked and read. Taylor couldn't remember afterwards exactly what they talked about. Current affairs. The state of the nation. Global warming.

It was easy not to be too worried about global warming, she thought, when the temperature was ten degrees below outside and you were wondering whether the candles were going to last out until the power was restored. But the discussion was stimulating nevertheless, like their discussions in the early days always had been, and it was all right if they kept to safe, impersonal subjects. She could go along with that.

When dusk fell they lit a couple of the candles and drew the curtains to shut out the winter's night.

They cooked potatoes for supper on the open fire, listening to them sizzle, inhaling their increasingly delicious aroma as they cooked. Then they cut wedges of crumbling cheese and buttered the soft white flesh of the halved potatoes, watching them run golden with black flecks from the melted butter and the crisp, disintegrating layers of the charcoaled skins.

Jared produced a red wine that was too cold at first but which grew warmer standing, uncorked, on the hearth.

'The snow ploughs were out in the valley.' Glass in hand, he had just dropped down to join her in front of the fire, having finished his meal on the settee. She had been too snug to move from the rug, and now she wished she had.

'I know.' She had seen them, way down on the flat white plane that formed the very mouth of Borrowdale, or at least seen the work that they were doing, watched over by the harsh faces of the imposing fells.

'It could be days before they get to us up here.'

She looked at him quickly. Her eyes were dark and guarded.

'What are you thinking?' In the flickering candlelight his mouth took on a sardonic curve. 'That it couldn't have worked out better if I'd planned it?'

She shrugged, trying to appear nonchalant. 'You're so scheming, Jared, it wouldn't have surprised me if you had.'

He had shaved finally, earlier in the day, but now that dark shadow was appearing again around his mouth and jaw so that in the subdued and dancing light his features took on an almost formidable attraction, as menacing as the cruel heights of the scree-scarred fells.

'Believe me. Improvising round a camp-fire wasn't exactly what I had in mind,' he told her, pushing a charred log back into the flames with the poker and a scintillating spray of sparks.

'What exactly did you plan?'

Pursing his lips, he set the glass he had just drained down on the hearth beside her. 'To wine and dine you in the best hotels Cumbria has to offer. For you to enjoy your holiday.'

Taylor cocked her head to one side, her eyes still wary. 'Why? To try to tempt me into coming back to you?'

He shrugged. 'Let's just say for old times' sake if you prefer.'

For old times' sake...

Broodingly her gaze roamed over the mason-cut stone of the fire surround, lifting to the old clock ticking peacefully away in the centre of the mantelpiece. Beside it, on either side, antique figurines and plates bore testimony to a gentler age—a slower, less materialistic world. Like those framed drawings she had penned and he had hung in the recesses bore testimony to a happier time, Taylor thought with a sudden wave of nostalgia for those days washing over her with such unexpected force that determinedly she uttered, trying to stay afloat, 'No, not for old times' sake. Anyway, we were always fighting.'

'Not always,' he said softly.

She couldn't look at him, knowing she would see in his eyes the same fervent emotion that thickened his voice. But, try though she did, she couldn't stamp out the memories of her own traitorous desires. They sprung out at her, sensual and erotic, from the darkest corners of her mind, of wild, uninhibited nights when, scored by his verbal lashings she had turned away from him in bed, only to be dragged unceremoniously into his arms where hurt, anger and pain had turned to lust as dark and desperate as their rows had been. Because how could it have been anything but lust—on either of their parts—when it had been born out of such bitter words and scarring accusations? she wondered, shamed now even to think how wantonly she had abandoned herself to him.

'That's all in the past,' she said and got quickly to her feet. Warmed by wine and the fire she felt a little bit woozy. 'I think I'll go to bed,' she told him, collecting up some of the dishes to take them outside.

'Don't jump down my throat when I suggest this, but why don't you share my room?' he said. 'It's not warm by any means but the fire's heated the chimney-breast and at least it's taken the chill off the air. Your room was like an icebox when I went in there this afternoon.'

His offer was tempting. So was the desire to give in to the pangs of wanting that just being with him had stirred in her ever since he had ploughed back into her life. But pride, or common sense, or whatever it was prevailed and she said primly, 'No thanks. I'll be perfectly all right where I am.'

'Suit yourself,' he said noncommittally and, picking up the bottle, poured a little more wine into his glass, his movements measured and steady, Taylor noted, as though he couldn't have cared one way or the other.

He was right about the bedroom though, she realised a little later after cleaning her teeth by candlelight in the equally cold bathroom. It was positively freezing!

She could see her breath on the air in the flickering yellow light as she hurriedly undressed and pulled on her short and less than substantial tunic of a nightdress.

Pale lemon, with a deep V-neck, cap sleeves and cutaway sides that left much of her thighs bare, it was something she had packed for a centrally heated bedroom, not the toe-nipping jaws of near Arctic conditions!

Blowing out the candle, she scrambled quickly into bed and, pulling the heavy duvet up around her, curled up into a tight ball. She lay like that for a long time with her teeth chattering, hoping to get warm, until her feet grew so numb she was forced to move to try rubbing them together. The bottom of the bed was freezing and her feet were like two blocks of ice!

Sometime later she heard Jared come up to bed. Always one to sleep with her bedroom door open, Taylor watched the flickering light of the candle he carried sending eerie shadows across her bedroom walls. Then he went into his own room and closed the door, plunging her into darkness once more.

'Pig,' she murmured under her breath, knowing he wouldn't be shivering like she was. He scarcely felt the cold beneath all that sinewy muscle and he could easily have offered to have taken her room when he had informed her of how cold it was. Instead of which he had expected that she would lightly take herself off to bed with him!

Restlessly she turned over, tugging the duvet grudgingly around her. She heard Jared moving about in the room across the landing; water running in the *en suite*, then the sound of the big bed creaking as he got in.

She didn't know how long she lay there awake and shivering, certainly long after he had fallen asleep, she was sure. At one point, jumping out, she groped around in the darkness and the wardrobe for her grey overcoat and threw that down on the bed. She had to warm up soon, she thought, or she'd die of hypothermia!

More than once, worn down by circumstances and the strain of the past two days, she felt sleep start to claim her, only to find herself awake a few moments later, still shivering with the cold.

Wanting to use the bathroom, she lay there for some time, growing more and more awake while she tried to summon up the courage to get out of bed. Eventually, telling herself things weren't going to get any better no matter how long she lay there, she scrambled out and raced to the bathroom, darting back only to misjudge in the darkness the exact length of the ottoman that stood at the foot of the bed.

Stubbing her toe on one corner, she stumbled against it with an almighty clunk and then, hopping painfully, managed to grope her way along the duvet and dived back into bed, shuddering not only from the cold, now, but also from her numb and bruised toe.

Facing the window, with her eyelids screwed tightly shut against all the discomfort, she wasn't aware of anything else until she heard Jared ask deeply from the doorway, 'What is it? What the devil's going on? Are you all right?'

'No.' Her teeth were chattering so much she could barely speak. 'I can't stop shivering,' she admitted, past caring now.

'You little fool.' A few swift strides brought him across the room.

Without wasting any time he was ripping back the duvet.

'Come here,' he growled, sliding in beside her, and with that he was pulling her into his arms.

CHAPTER SIX

His body was hard and warm as he turned her into him, its merciful heat enveloping her, seeping through into every last shivering cell.

If he had been wearing a T-shirt when he had come in, then he must have pulled it off to give her the maximum benefit of his body temperature, Taylor thought with a violent shudder, crushed against the crisp dark hair that furred the deep contours of his chest.

He was wearing shorts in some soft, stretchy fabric that left no mystery about his potent manhood, and she could feel the roughness of his hair-covered legs as they entwined with the smooth cool silk of hers.

'That better?' he asked hoarsely.

It was. She couldn't tell him how much, and all she could do was groan her gratitude from within his powerful embrace.

His broad back felt like warm velvet beneath her clinging fingers, and she could feel the play of powerful muscle beneath the smooth skin. He smelt good too, of cedar and a familiar underlying musk that had her nostrils dilating, greedy for as much of his warm scent as they could hold.

'You shouldn't have got that cold.' His tone was lightly abrasive. 'You should have come in and told me.'

'You were asleep,' she argued by means of a feeble excuse. Already she was feeling better. His body was like a furnace and the bed was becoming nicely warm at last.

'No, I wasn't.'

Wasn't he? Against the warm satin of his shoulder, her

brow puckered. Why not? What had kept him awake? 'I didn't want to disturb you.'

She felt the deep wall of his chest expand slightly. 'Evidently not,' he scolded, releasing a curiously ragged breath.

A small satisfied sigh escaped Taylor. She had stopped shivering at last. In fact, she was virtually glowing now.

'Warmer?' His voice was a lilting caress against her hair.

She murmured an affirmation, and suddenly realised that it wasn't just his proximity that was warming her blood. Inside her something stirred, something born out of hunger and denial that her body recognised, and to which it was responding, seemingly with a will of its own.

From somewhere in the depths of her consciousness a little voice was struggling to be heard, but her ears were deaf to its futile warning.

She caught the shuddering breath that Jared drew and at the same time became aware of her own shallow breathing, knew that he had to have noticed it too.

Way down in the centre of her abdomen she felt the deep throb of desire, felt its molten message pierce her loins, her aching flesh, the tightening aureoles of her small breasts.

Pulled by something beyond her own volition, she moved restlessly against him, her legs unconsciously massaging the coarse length of his, her body thrilling to the full exciting knowledge of his arousal.

'Taylor...' It sounded like a growl, or a hopeless plea, she wasn't sure which. She only knew that whatever she was feeling, he was feeling it too.

She could almost touch the leashed power of his aggressive virility, the tight-wire tension that packed every nerve and sinew of his body.

For a fraction of a second, her self-preservation shrieked at her to draw back, but it was already too late.

As he groaned, then pushed her on to her back, her

senses were already leaping to meet their own destruction and when his mouth came down over hers she arched towards him with a stifled cry, lost in a conflagration of her own need.

Oh, dear heaven! How had she lived without this!

The stubble of his jaw was abrasive on her skin, rough and unbearably arousing, while their mouths blended, breathless and devouring, demanding a deeper knowledge of the other that each knew could only be reached in the most elemental way.

Shudders racked her body as his hard hands slid under the soft fabric of her tunic, seeking, claiming, kneading the slender curves of her eager hips. His massaging fingers moved to splay across the small span of her waist, and Taylor caught her breath as they slid along her ribcage to trace, with tantalising skill, the outer edges of her breasts.

He was and always had been a consummate lover, knowing exactly when to make her wait and when to grant her pleasure. But now she sucked in a breath, moving convulsively against him. How could he deny her when she wanted him so much!

'Oh God...' he breathed as though she strained his self-control, and slid his hands over her breasts now as reverently as if he were fondling priceless treasures.

'Jared...' It was a small sobbed sound, torn from her as he slid down and pushed back her tunic so that his mouth could close over one breast, his fingers caressing and moulding and teasing the other into throbbing tumescence before his mouth claimed that one too, drawing it into its erotically suckling warmth, sending an agony of exquisite pleasure down through her lower body.

Her fingers were luxuriating in the thickness of his hair, both hands eagerly caressing him, reacquainting themselves with the curve of his head, the coarser hair that formed his sideburns, the hard, exciting structure of his cheek and jaw.

Little murmurs of pleasure escaped her as his lips and hands rediscovered her, spasms bringing her straining against him—this man of whom she could never have enough—inviting, accepting him as sole licensee of her body.

She could feel the fullness of his arousal pressing against her beneath the soft shorts and she wanted to be rid of the barrier, wanted him inside of her, guiding her, controlling her, taking her with him to some other place, some other part of the universe that no one else could share.

She grappled with his waistband, slid her hand beneath it and felt the tightening flesh of a firm buttock. But then he reached down and helped her, pulling the garment free, then tugged her tunic over her head so that they were lying naked together.

The air in the room was like ice on her sensitised body, but that didn't matter any more. Heat seared her as he came back down to her, causing her to gasp from the electrifying sensation of his warm nakedness.

This was where she belonged! This was where she had always belonged, she told herself feverishly, with no thought for tomorrow. In this man's arms. In his bed. Giving as much as he demanded of her. And taking too. Taking in turn.

With his lower body pressed against hers, tantalising her with the promise of unbearable pleasure, he lay propped up on his elbows, hesitating, as though gripped by a moment's doubt, like an undeserving soul unsure whether to take or turn away from the unexpected gift of heaven.

In the darkness, desperately Taylor's eyes sought his.

Was he harbouring second thoughts? He couldn't be. She *was* his and there was nothing she could do about it except take him into her, she reasoned blindly, thrusting her pelvis towards his.

As if that one action had snapped his self-control, he was

pushing hard into her, the sudden and rapturous reality of his filling her drawing guttural sobs from her throat.

She was moving with him, joining him in a rhythm that was theirs and had only ever been theirs alone. She felt him sink deeper into her and she moved to accommodate him, winding her legs around him and gripping him hard, locking him to her in a dizzying, primeval rhapsody of the senses.

He groaned, robbed of his powers to do anything but lose himself to the generously offered gift of her femininity. But she had already begun to climax from the powerful thrusts of his body, and she felt the moist warmth of his flowing into her, first as an aphrodisiac, increasing her pleasure, then as a soothing balm after the fierce and throbbing contractions of her own body.

The next thing she knew it was morning. Sunlight was streaming in through a chink in the curtains and Jared's side of the bed was empty.

The cold struck home as she slipped an arm out of the bed, and she quickly retracted it, reminded all too shockingly that she was naked.

Shame stung her more than the icy temperature in the room. Why had she let him? Let herself? she wondered despairingly. Why, whenever he was around, could she never constrain herself? Retain any self-control? She gritted her teeth, angry with herself. How could she have behaved so recklessly, when nothing had been resolved between them, and the only reason for his coming here had been to seduce her back into his bed—into his life—regardless of what she wanted? Of what was best for her?

Even now, lying here with regret and shame as her bed partners, her swollen breasts were tingling from the memory of his kneading hands, the sensual throb at the core of her femininity from just thinking about him assuring her that if he came in now her body would open to him again as a flower opens to the sun, welcoming him into her; that she could only ever be whole and fully alive with this man as her lover.

She got up quickly, slung on her dressing gown and darted into the bathroom, ignoring the biting chill while she forced herself to wash in the bitterly cold water.

Downstairs, dressed in a black polo-necked sweater, thick shirt and jeans, she had started washing the dishes from the previous night with water from the kettle she had found already singing on the fire when the back door opened with a blast of cold air and Jared stood there, kicking snow off his boots.

'Morning,' he greeted her somewhat cautiously, coming in.

'Morning,' Taylor returned quietly, with half a glance over her shoulder, unable to look at him, not only because she felt too ashamed, but also because, if she had, she knew exactly what she would have seen. A dark, unshaven Jared sporting that brutish man-of-the-fells image in his thick country clothes and padded body warmer, and she was having enough difficulty keeping her anxiety over the previous night reined in, without letting him see how potently she was affected by him as well.

'The power's still off, as you've probably gathered.' He was opening a cupboard, putting something away. 'And there's no sign of a thaw.'

Taylor swirled hot suds around a plate with the washing-up brush. 'No.' The residue of last night's feast had set hard on the china, refusing to be erased. Like their love-making, she thought, keeping her head down and scrubbing hard.

'At least we haven't had any fresh snowfall.'

'Haven't we?' She sounded disenchanted but she couldn't help it.

After a marked hesitation, he said, 'Did you put the kettle back on to boil?'

'Yes,' she answered, wondering why he appeared so coldly matter-of-fact. Was he recriminating himself for what had happened last night? Was he regretting it too?

Behind her the cupboard door banged. 'Did you sleep well?'

Taylor scrubbed at the caked potato more violently. 'Yes.'

'No more problems with being cold?'

Was he kidding?

'No,' she said tautly, her actions mirroring her agitation. Well, how else was she expected to feel? Last night they had both behaved recklessly and he wasn't even mentioning it, which made the whole thing even more disconcerting.

'For heaven's sake, save your energy,' he said, suddenly sounding impatient, 'and leave that blasted plate to soak.'

She dropped it abruptly. It made a dull clunk as it hit the bottom of the sink.

'What's wrong?' He was opening the cutlery drawer, making its contents rattle as he rammed it closed again. His voice wasn't too gentle. 'Worried you might be pregnant?'

She winced, because of course the thought had crossed her mind but it wasn't just that. She hadn't agreed to go back with him because, as far as she was concerned, nothing had changed. He would still love Alicia, no matter how much he convinced himself he couldn't have her—that it was over. It was another man's wife he really wanted to be the woman at his side. But last night, just as in the past, when he made love to her, she couldn't think straight; tried to make herself believe that she meant more to him than just a substitute for someone else. Last night had been no exception because he had made love to her as though his heart and mind were free for him to do so—unreservedly and uninhibitedly—and she had let him, practically instigating it, while knowing that sooner rather than later they would become just another statistic in the eternal line of broken marriages, because she could never go back to him to be what she had been to him before, just a convenient little stand-in for somebody else.

And now, of course, because of her foolish and utterly thoughtless behaviour, there was the worry, as he'd said, that she could be pregnant...

'It shouldn't have happened,' she demurred, staring at the cup she was washing without even seeing it.

'That's obvious,' he said brusquely, behind her.

'I don't want to be pregnant,' she protested, fighting the idea, her deep buried fears surfacing above everything else.

'No,' he breathed heavily in acceptance. 'You made your opinions and objections clear enough while we were living together. I should have known better. I could easily have used something. But then neither of us was in the mood for rational thinking, were we? Well, what's done is done, Taylor. We can't put the clock back. And if you are carrying my child, I'm sure you'll work something out where it doesn't inconvenience you too much.'

'Like I did the last time?' She spun round to face him with the washing-up brush in her hand, soapsuds flying everywhere. Her teeth were clenched from the pain of remembering, her green eyes over-bright with bitter emotion. 'Isn't that what you accused me of? Getting rid of our unborn child?'

'No!' He was dragging a hand across his cheek, wiping away suds from where she had splashed him. Soapy water ran down the dark shiny front of his body warmer. 'I never said that.'

'No? Only that losing our baby was exactly what I wanted!'

With his wide shoulders held rigid, jaw locked tight,

there was a bleak look about him as though remembering pained him too.

'It was a…natural…assumption…' he said, picking his words carefully '…in view of the way you were…the way you seemed to have no time for…' He broke off on a heavily drawn breath. 'For heaven's sake, Taylor! Do I have to spell it out?'

No, he didn't, she thought, turning around again, her brush toying absently with the winking bubbles in the bowl.

Throughout her short marriage, she had shied away from any contact with babies, refusing to show any interest in them; wanting one so desperately she couldn't bear to inflame the need. Jared had scorned her lack of maternal instinct, but he had been unaware of her fears, taking her attitude as a total disregard—if not distaste—for children and motherhood, which was why he had been so derisive when he had seen her with Josh.

Her pregnancy had been the result of an impassioned row, a making up during which, just as the previous night, neither had had the will nor the inclination to consider protection. She remembered the first tentative excitement she had experienced—the joy even—when she had first suspected that she was going to have a baby; then, when it was confirmed, the fear. She became withdrawn and introverted. Moody, too, she accepted with a mental grimace. So it probably wasn't that surprising that he had picked up on those vibes; why he thought she was no less than relieved when he came home from that ten-day conference and she told him that she had miscarried.

Numbly, she shook her head. No, he didn't have to spell it out.

'Don't feel so bad about it, Taylor,' he advised in a suddenly silken voice and she realised he was talking about last night. 'Neither of us could have prevented it, and the way we are whenever we're around each other...well, it was bound to happen sooner or later.'

'Why? Because you were determined it would?'

He laughed softly behind her. 'Hopeful, dearest, but not exactly determined.'

'OK. So you got what you wanted.'

'What *I* wanted?' he breathed with harsh emphasis and, before she could sidestep, he was reaching out and pulling her back against the whipcord strength of his body. 'What *I* wanted,' he repeated, his words softly mocking now because his arms were already crossed over her breasts, and his hands were massaging the small mounds through her clinging sweater. 'I think, my love, if I took you upstairs now, you'd be begging me again as helplessly as you were begging me last night.' The reminder stung, scorching her cheeks with bright colour. 'You want me as much as I want you—no matter how much your pride and crazy determination tell you otherwise. OK. Perhaps you were right once when you accused me of marrying you on the rebound. Maybe I didn't show you enough love or appreciate you as much as I should have done. Possibly I neglected to do all the little things you needed me to do for you to feel wanted—perhaps I *was* away too much. Oh, I'm not going to lie and say I wasn't still in contact with Alicia when I met you. God knows, I was!' His deep voice seemed to rumble with an intensity of emotion and, recognising it, Taylor closed her eyes against it, against the longing to be able to move him to such a degree. 'When I saw you at that party, you were like the promise of summer after a long, long winter, with your youth, your sexy mystique and your surprising innocence. You showed me something new, something different, something to hope for. And you excited me more than any woman I'd ever met.'

She wanted to keep her mind on what he was saying, hold on to her composure, but she couldn't because of what he was doing to her. Even through the layers of her clothes her breasts were responding to his sensuous massage, his sweet provocation stimulating the more intimate and secret pathways of her body.

'Give us this chance, Taylor.'

His lips against her ear whispered their trembling message, his teeth nipping the sensitive area now just above the neck of her sweater, so treacherously feather-light that she gave a small groan and dropped her head back against him.

'What you're suffering—what we're both suffering from,' he breathed, 'is chronic frustration from being cooped up here together. It's not surprising I'm going out of my mind with wanting you—with what I want to do *to* you. Especially when—deny it as you may, Taylor—you want it too.'

His breath came warmly across her ear, arousing her, bringing her hand up to the nape of his neck so that he wouldn't stop, because, dear Heaven! she wanted him to do all those things he had spoken of, take her upstairs and make her his again, so that she could make him hers, and only hers...

'No, Taylor,' he said gently, reading all the signals. 'That won't do either of us any good right now.' With amazing control he was removing her arm from around his neck, leaving her feeling oddly bereft and disappointed as his hands slid away from her. 'Right now—for both our sanities' sakes—I think you should concentrate on breakfast, while I finish off what I was doing outside. And then, my dearest, I'm yours for the rest of the day, during which you and I are going to get down to some really serious fun.'

CHAPTER SEVEN

'A TOBOGGAN!'

Taylor stared disbelievingly at the sleek, well-made contraption Jared had dragged around to the front of the house and thought back to his disturbing words in the kitchen earlier about having fun. 'You're never going to get two of us on that thing!' And when she could see that that was his intention, 'You're crazy!' she laughed.

From the other side of the narrow slatted frame, Jared gave a casual shrug. 'Possibly,' he conceded with a wry compression of lips, but she sensed a hidden depth of meaning in the way he said it.

'Where did you get it?' It was obvious he had dug the sledge out of the old shed. But then something rang a bell with her, even as he started to remind her. Just large enough to take two adults, at a push, he had constructed it himself under the keen eye of his grandfather when he had been a mere youngster. Its cleverly constructed design, though, with the painstaking curvature at its front, showed how good he was with his hands and what a talented, caring craftsman he might have been if he hadn't chosen to make his living with his brilliant intellect instead.

Like him she had already donned a thick anorak, woollen hat and gloves and scouted around for some wellingtons from a previous visit when he had suggested she get ready for a walk.

Now the green eyes she lifted to his were shining with anticipation and excitement. 'Well? Are you going to take me for a ride?'

So he did, laughing at her eagerness as they came out of

the lane and trudged, with the sledge trailing behind them,
up the frozen, steeply rising ground.

From the top of a long sweep of snow-blanched terrain
he stopped, and Taylor turned to look about her.

They had come a long way, much further than she had
expected. She couldn't see the house now, only the smoke
drifting up from its chimney above a belt of trees. Now
and again she caught the faintest traces of its sweet woody
scent on the air. Below it, on the flat pastures of the valley,
sheep huddled together, feeding on silage and hay, fat
woollen bundles, heavily pregnant with lambs, or with their
young already braving the unexpected freeze-up at their
mothers' sides. A tractor was moving away from them, out
of range of her hearing, and yet if she listened she could
almost imagine she could hear the throb of its engine on
the absolute stillness of the air.

Perhaps that was why the travel brochures and magazines
referred to this valley as the loveliest in England, Taylor
appreciated, allowing her eyes the luxury of a full breath-
taking survey.

Grey and white stone houses—clustered in hamlets—
crouched beside open fields and seasonally stark woodands,
a tranquil haven within the deep yawning mouth of the
mountains. She could see the meandering river glinting in
the sun, disappearing now beneath one of the many small
stone bridges that were a feature of the area, appearing
again between twisting, wooded banks, joining the dark
oval of Derwent Water on its south side with Bassenthwaite
Lake to the north. The low stone boundary walls of the
outer fields, she noticed, stretched to the very foothills of
the mountains, while beyond, at the head of the valley, the
dramatic assembly of craggy peaks dominated the whole
scene, austere, magnificent and awesome.

Like him, Taylor decided as her gaze came back to where
Jared was stooping, doing something to the toboggan.

Behind him their own mountainside glared down at them, its face cruel and inclement, giving no quarter to the unwary hiker.

He would know every curve and bend of these hillsides, she thought, with a marked degree of respect for him; know which ones to traverse and which to avoid. And it surprised her to realise that she didn't doubt for one second that she would be safe with him. That in spite of all that had happened, between them, she would trust him with her very life if she had to.

A small frisson ran through her just from the sight of his bent head in the dark wool hat, from watching him securing the tow-ropes and thinking about what those capable gloved hands could do to her.

Suddenly then he stood up, caught her looking at him through the dark glasses he had recommended they both should wear and colour stained her cheeks, already pink with the cold.

'OK.' With sighed resignation she dropped a swift glance to the sledge, before meeting those shielded dark eyes again. 'Thrill me,' she purred huskily, slipping her hands into her pockets.

It was the worst thing she could have said, of course. Or the best, she thought, depending on which way she wanted to look at it, because if he had been intending to break her in gently to the experience of tobogganing then, after that rather foolhardy challenge, all his reservations went by the wayside.

'I'll make you scream,' he promised excitingly, as she clambered onto the wooden slats in front of him, and he proceeded to do just that, laughing at her shrieks as he nudged them off the top of the slope to bring them flying down the hillside at a startling pace.

Faster and faster they seemed to go, gathering momentum as they descended so that she wondered if they would ever be able to stop.

'I can't believe this! How can you do this to me?' she screamed above the rush of steel over the ice, shrieking even more loudly as the toboggan hit a bump, then another, so that she bounced back against him, laughing hysterically.

It was a tight squeeze sitting there between his legs with her own legs drawn up in front of her, and with her hands gripping the sides of the sledge as if her life depended on it, although she had no worries on that score.

Caught between Jared's hard thighs and those powerful arms clutching the ropes, she was vibrantly aware of his strength and the solid padding of his body both ready to protect her if she did take a tumble.

All around them free-roaming sheep with brightly painted rumps stared after them as they sailed past, and Taylor laughed at their bemused faces, catching their tremulous chorus of bleats through the rush of the cold clean air.

'You rotten…!' Swearing amicably, she was still laughing as they ploughed into a deep drift and came to a sudden halt, sending white flakes flying everywhere. 'You made it bump deliberately!'

'No, I didn't.'

'Yes, you did,' she argued. 'You singled them out just to pay me back.'

'So what if I did? You asked for it,' he reminded her wickedly, arguing back. Like children, she thought. Without a care in the world.

'I could have come off.'

'No you couldn't.' His thighs tightened on either side of her, emphasising his point. 'Only if *I* did,' he murmured silkily, 'and the worst you could have experienced would have been a roll in the snow.'

His murmured approval of the idea suddenly made

Taylor disturbingly conscious of the powerful legs entrapping her, of the strong arm around her middle and the warmth of his breath fanning her cold cheek when she sent him a challenging glance over her shoulder.

'OK.' He lifted his hands, palms outwards in acceptance. 'So you don't share the same view.'

He was laughing down at her, the glare of the sun, with the brilliance of the snow bouncing off his dark glasses, accentuating every line and curve of his magnificent bone structure, the hard-etched jaw and forehead, that proud straight nose, the gleaming whiteness of his teeth.

He was different here, she thought. Different from the hard-headed, hard-working and often disdainful entrepreneur who had had far too little time for her back in London and who, when he had found time to be with her, had scared her witless with his brilliance and his power over her mind and body. But here she hadn't even seen him using his mobile phone.

Here he was fun to be with—was taking time to relax— and for the first time she was seeing a new and exciting playfulness in him that unsettled as much as it pleased her. She wasn't ready just to shelve all her fears and her anxieties and go back to him, and she was worried that this sudden absolute interest in her—his decision to give her all his undivided attention—was just a ploy to get her back; that, once there, their marriage would revert to being the same insecure and tumultuous farce that it had been before.

'No,' she assured him firmly, negating his suggestion— however flippant—of any further intimacy between them, even though her body throbbed and her breath came quickly through her lungs just from thinking about it. 'It just complicates things,' she said.

For a moment those hard thighs gripping hers tightened inexorably. Another glance over her shoulder revealed how the bright sun made a hard, cruel feature of his mouth.

What was he thinking? she wondered hectically, scanning the sudden, stark rigidity of his face. But then almost at once his features relaxed, as did his hold on her.

'Come on,' he rasped, springing to his feet a second after she did. 'Let's get this thing back up the hill.'

After that the morning resumed most of its earlier conviviality for which Taylor was relieved. She didn't want to be forced to look too closely at her feelings for him. She wanted to enjoy these moments together without any pressure from him.

There was tension in her laughter now though as she travelled, clinging to his long legs, down the crisp cold hill, even when she fell off in an unharmed, shrieking heap with him, and emerged from her fall, pelting him with snow. There was also circumspection in the way he touched her, as though he were avoiding any reoccurrence of what had transpired between them the previous night.

They were lovers who had just crossed a threshold and become what they knew they should be. What they really were. Estranged partners, she thought painfully, dusting snow off her anorak and track suit bottoms. Strangers, shackled together merely by bad weather and by that keen astuteness of Jared's in knowing that she would come.

She straightened suddenly, a hand shielding her eyes—in spite of her sunglasses—as her ears registered the continuously mournful bleating some distance away.

'What is it?' Jared was beside her, brushing snow from his shoulder. His shielded gaze followed hers to the stream winding down towards the valley, its swollen silver waters tumbling between craggy banks.

'I don't know. A lamb in distress. It keeps calling but there's nothing answering,' Taylor said, concerned.

'Probably been a bit too adventurous and like most kids preferred to ignore sound parental advice,' Jared murmured dryly, but Taylor was only half listening.

She could see it now, down by the beck, its small cloven feet slipping over icy stones, its black-hooded face lifting with each cry that came piercingly on the air.

'There it is!' she said, pointing to the spot between two overhanging trees where the river-bank curved steeply.

'It's been born too early for all this savage weather,' Jared commented sympathetically.

'It's all alone.' Taylor's face was puckered with worry. 'We should rescue it.'

'No, we shouldn't,' he contradicted her, and as she made to move past him, 'Leave it,' he advised with a restraining hand on her arm. 'They have voice-boxes like radar,' he assured her. 'Its mother will find it. Every ewe is instinctively tuned to the call of its young.'

From behind their dark lenses, wounded and sceptical eyes flew accusingly to his.

'She'll come back for him,' he promised.

'But supposing she doesn't?' With all her strength she was pushing him aside, leaving him staggering backwards.

'Taylor! Taylor, don't be stupid! For pity's sake! It's treacherous down there!'

Drawn by the animal's cries, she took no heed of Jared's angry warning, stumbling over steep and slippery ground, her only thought, somehow to help the distressed creature.

Teetering down the bank towards the beck, she managed to stop herself by grasping frantically at the overhanging branch of a tree just before her sliding feet almost plunged her into the water.

'Heck.' It was a small gasp of relief at having saved herself from Jared's scorn rather than an icy soaking. She wasn't sure which would have stung most, but she could guess.

Taking a dim view of her sudden crashing into its sphere, the lamb, however, had leaped further up the bank, bleating now with fear and indignation.

From a few metres away, it stood shaking on its spindly legs, little face turned towards her, bleating pitifully.

'Come on. I won't hurt you.' Finding a safe footing at last, stooping to make herself appear less threatening, Taylor murmured soft little coaxing phrases above the tumbling of the stream. 'Come on, little sheep. Don't be afraid.'

It looked frightened and cold—and was probably very hungry too, she thought, her heart going out to it standing there, lost and defenceless, with its little legs half buried in a drift of snow.

And suddenly she could feel its fear; feel the cold that numbed her own feet and the cruel wind penetrating her bones as though she weren't protected by her gloves, thick socks and anorak because memory was stripping her of those defences, stripping back the years so that she was five years old again, shivering, vulnerable and afraid.

She didn't hear Jared shout, catching only the stronger-voiced vibrato of the ewe that was standing, viewing Taylor suspiciously from above the river-bank, bleating her impatience with her errant offspring.

Recognising its mother, the lamb leaped into the air as if on wires, making short work now of the slippery slope. There was a joyous cacophony of bleats before the small hooded face nudged under it mother's thick coat, tail wagging from the warm comfort of her milk.

In only a few seconds, though, the ewe was pulling away from the small questing mouth, urging her lamb to safety and more familiar ground.

Jared was right, Taylor thought with a cold emotion shuddering through her, staring after the bright disappearing rump of the ewe with her skittish, reunited lamb. Even an animal came back for its young.

'What the hell did you think you were doing dashing—' Strong arms were turning her roughly, the deep male voice breaking off as those shaded eyes tugged questioningly over her finely drawn features.

'What is it?' he asked urgently. 'What's wrong, Taylor?' He was reaching up to remove her glasses, using his other hand to make her look at him when she tried to turn away. With infinite tenderness his thumb moved across the pale, drawn lines of her face, over the sadness of her downturned mouth. 'What is it?' he whispered, concerned.

His touch and the tone of his voice were so gentle and so moving after his anger of a few moments ago that she pressed her eyelids closed against the sensations that were running riot in her, struggling to bring her emotions under control.

'Just me getting too sentimental over an animal,' she exhaled heavily, opening her eyes.

Above the dark glasses, she saw the black brows come together, noticed his interest shift to the retreating ewe and her lamb before returning to Taylor again, and now the furrow deepened between his eyes.

'Tell me,' he commanded quietly, unconvinced, drawing a soft leather finger down the curve of her cheek.

For a moment, recognising the depth of understanding—of tenderness—in him, she wanted to open up, share her innermost fears, feeling them being drawn from her by those shielded, searching eyes. But instead came the shocking recognition of just how much she still loved him—that she had never stopped loving him! That she could so easily believe him when he said his affair with Alicia was over with, before they were married, because she wanted to—so much! Which would mean, if that *were* the case, that it had all been her fault that her marriage had failed, wouldn't it? she thought suddenly, because she hadn't trusted him enough. Because she couldn't hold on to anything...

You'll always run away.

'Take me home,' she uttered quickly on a series of violent shivers. 'For heaven's sake, let's go back. I'm freezing.'

They had potatoes on the fire again for lunch with ham and pickles, and a huge helping of fresh fruit to follow.

Now, having fallen asleep on the settee, relaxed by the fire and the unaccustomed amount of exercise she had taken that morning, Taylor woke to the jangle of brass rings and realised that Jared was closing the heavy curtains. On the mantelpiece, she noted, he had already lit the candles. She could smell the wax, and noticed that one was burning rather erratically where there wasn't much of it left.

'Awake at last.' His voice was warm, indulgent.

Taylor sat up, putting her feet on the floor.

'What time is it?' she wanted to know, her hand stifling a yawn.

'What does it matter?' Jared came around the settee, looking down at her from his advantageous position. 'We aren't going anywhere.'

A small thread of excitement needled its way rapidly through her, jabbing alive feelings that were hot and sensual, piercing others with poignant regret.

No, she was snowbound here in a private world with this man who could make her blood sing with the potency of his sexuality; who could make her respond to his will because she was so crazy about him, and who had asked her to give them a chance. But if she did and they started afresh, together, then the pressures would be on her again...

'I must have fallen asleep,' she said, stating the obvious.

'That comes from taking too much exercise you're not used to. Both this morning—' He broke off, that sensual compression of his lips finishing the sentence. *And last night.*

She turned away from those penetrating eyes and was glad when he went over and started stoking up the fire.

Surreptitiously, she watched the play of muscle beneath the thick check shirt he was wearing as he stooped to toss the last of the logs from the wicker basket into the flames. There was a book lying open, face down, on the easy chair opposite her. A book about the English Civil War, she noted, remembering his penchant for English history. So he had been reading while she slept, she realised, the thought of the rather homely scene giving a sudden violent tug on her heartstrings.

'I wish the power would come back on.' Distractedly she ran a hand through her dishevelled hair. He had made her run for a large part of the way home, forcing her blood to pump through her after he had seen her shivering down by the beck and now she felt decidedly grubby. 'I'd give anything for a bath.' Even if she could have managed to heat sufficient water on the fire to give her a bare amount to bathe in, there was no way, she decided, that she could face the temperature of the cold, unheated bathroom. Not while there were still subzero temperatures outside!

His countenance was grim as he picked up the log basket to refill it and went out, saying nothing. He probably felt the same way, unless he was taking cold showers—which she wouldn't have put past him, Taylor decided with a grimace, until she remembered that even that was an impossibility without any electricity. Nevertheless, she wished she had kept her mouth shut, hoping she hadn't sounded as though she had been complaining unnecessarily when he was doing his best to make them both comfortable.

Resigned to her discomfort, she got up and started clearing the dishes left over from lunchtime, filled the kettle for more water to wash them and with a small shudder went back to the warm sitting room where the logs Jared had heaped on the fire were already glowing red, giving off extra heat.

Roll on the thaw, Taylor thought wryly, placing the kettle across the two little walls of bricks that Jared had found in the shed and ingeniously erected in the grate for that very purpose before lighting the fire that morning. He had made the whole experience of being snowed in easier than it would have been had she simply been here on her own, she reflected with reluctant honesty. OK, she would probably have coped, though a little less efficiently since she lacked his degree of physical strength for chopping logs and suchlike, but she had to admit that Jared had somehow managed to make it fun. Even so, it was still harder work than she was used to, and it certainly made her appreciate how difficult life must have been for the ordinary people a century or so earlier, but that didn't stop her longing to get back to normality. Just to be able to feel clean again, she thought, if for no other reason, because a thaw would mean going home—returning to her safe, self-sufficient existence, and as much as she knew that the sooner that happened and she could get away from Jared, the better it would be for her, some crazy, aching part of her—the part that loved him—didn't want this time with him ever to end.

She had just finished lighting a candle on the mantelpiece, replacing the one that had finally burned itself out, when a thud against the door jamb had her turning quickly.

Wearing the anorak he had casually thrown on to go outside, Jared was manoeuvring a large oval tin bath through the doorway.

'I don't believe this!' Taylor laughed incredulously.

Seeing him trying to kick the rug aside with his booted foot, Taylor rushed to help him, dragging the table to one side and folding the rug clear of the space between the chair and the sofa so that he could set the hollow oval tub down in front of the fire.

'There you are.' He ran his hand around the tub's interior, brushing out some foreign objects. 'Every modern convenience.'

Still amazed, Taylor stared down at it. 'How are we going to heat enough water to fill that?'

'As your forebears did, darling. With one kettleful after another. Bath night, I believe, was every Friday or Saturday night.'

'In front of the fire.' Right now it sounded like pure luxury. *In front of him.*

Disconcerted, she uttered, 'Did your grandparents use this? Did you?' Try though she did, she couldn't imagine him living quite so rustically.

He laughed, and said, confirming it, 'Good heavens no! *I* didn't. There was always the bathroom—certainly in my time. I'm not sure this was ever used. It did, however, come in useful for mixing potting compost and keeping goldfish outside in during the summer months.'

'You're joking!' Horrified green eyes lifted from the ancient metal to meet those that were deep-set, dark and definitely laughing at her. 'Thanks,' she chided dryly, secretly amused.

Having to wait for each kettleful of water, it took some time to fill the bath to a practical level—until Jared found a large cauldron in the old pantry and started heating the water in that instead.

With the bath almost ready and steaming invitingly, Taylor went to fetch some of the toiletries she had brought with her; soap from the bathroom and, still in its paper bag, the bottle of fragrant bath foam she had purchased when she and Craig and another member of the crew had gone on a shopping expedition in Edinburgh a few days before.

She was glad Jared was upstairs, moving around in the master bedroom when she came back down because, intimate though they had been during their marriage and then shockingly—her cheeks burned as she thought about it— the previous night, she felt absurdly self-conscious in the present circumstances about undressing in front of him.

She quickly discarded her clothes and, sweeping her hair up and securing it with a large clasp she had brought down with her, she stepped nimbly into the water.

With her shoulders supported by one end of the bath and her long legs draped over the other, she was luxuriating with her eyes closed—breasts barely covered—in the scented bubbles when he strode back in.

She wasn't sure if he had sat down or if he had gone back out of the room because she couldn't hear him moving around and she felt too relaxed to open her eyes and look. There was no sound but the crackling of logs on the fire, the soft pup-pup of bubbles dispersing in the foam and a strange kind of fizzing she was straining her ears to identify.

Something cool and smooth skimmed her leg, and she gasped, drawing it up sharply, her eyes flying open to the realisation of Jared standing there above her, that it was the cool base of a crystal glass flute he had been trailing along her leg.

'Champagne?' she beamed, surprised.

'I never travel without it.'

He had changed, she noticed, into a soft black shirt and black corduroys, an image, which, with his black hair and those glittering black eyes rocked her with its sexual impact.

'You're decadent,' she accused in a voice that faltered, reaching up and taking the glass from him.

'If you mean in the sense of being self-indulgent, then I can only admit to being entirely guilty of that,' he accepted. 'But if you mean in the sense that I'm morally corrupt, then no man could apologise for dispensing with his highest principles around you, Taylor.'

What did he mean by that exactly?

Guardedly, with loose strands curling damply against her face, she watched him retrieve his own glass from the mantelpiece then, with one easy stretch of his body, pick up the book he had been reading earlier and cross to the settee.

Was he, she wondered, in some way alluding to last night? Was he, like her, and in spite of everything he had said, somehow regretting what had happened?

Refusing to think about that, she savoured the champagne, considering, as she twisted the slim stem of the glass how ridiculous it seemed sipping the most expensive wine from what looked like incredibly valuable crystal while lying in a battered tin tub!

'Why the Madonna smile?'

That deep voice sliced through her reverie, bringing her head round.

He was sitting with his book lying open on the palm of his hand, one long leg lying across the other, those thoughtful eyes watching her as a Roman emperor would have watched his naked and favourite slave girl, as though she amused and entertained him.

'What were you thinking of?'

Head tilting, Taylor surveyed the leaping fire through the carved perfection of the crystal, noting the way the one filled and impregnated every last fine sculpted contour of the other.

'Incongruities,' she murmured, taking another sip.

'Such as?'

'This.' She held up her glass. 'And this.' A toss of her chin indicated the bathtub. 'You and I.'

'You and—' She couldn't look at him sitting there with the book, still open, but transferred to his lap now. His left arm was stretched across the back of the settee. 'What are you saying? That we're that much of a mismatch? Out of harmony with one another? Incompatible?' When she didn't answer, but just went on sipping her champagne, he said, 'There is one way, my love, where you and I certainly aren't incompatible, and if you're determined to make that sort of rash remark then I'll just have to—'

She was both relieved—and surprised—when the phone on the little round table beside the settee started to ring. Just how they got on in bed was something of which she certainly didn't need reminding!

It was a business call, she deduced almost immediately, discarding her glass on the other low table she just managed to reach behind her, before lying back and listening to the deep sensuality of his voice.

'No, it's switched off,' he was saying, obviously referring to his mobile phone. 'No, I shan't be dealing with it. I've left Steve Shaunessy in charge.'

His second in command. A big Irishman, Taylor remembered from the days when she had played hostess to Jared's business colleagues and their wives. Steve was clever, astute. Trustworthy. She hadn't forgotten, either, the sympathy she had seen in the man's eyes when he had looked at her sometimes, and had been sure that he was thinking what she had guessed they must all have been thinking—everyone who knew, that was—that she was only a young and callow substitute who Jared had married in place of someone else.

'Get Steve to deal with it,' he went on, with no mention that he was on leave, with whom, or how long he intended to be away, which only emphasised that, as head of a thriving company, he was answerable to no one.

He was speaking to a woman—probably his secretary—Taylor decided, simply from that certain tone he always used with the opposite sex. Just like everything else about him, his voice had the most profound effect on women. And Taylor Adams was no exception, she thought, resenting the way that, even now, when her spirits had plummeted just from remembering how she had felt during their marriage, when she had felt betrayed and second best, those deep tones were arousing her, grazing over her senses the way his shirt would graze her naked body, or his chest hair rasp against the sudden aching tightness of her breasts...

'No. Don't call me here again.'

Catching that impatient, dismissive note in his voice, mentally she shook herself out of her dangerous reverie before the phone clattered back onto its rest.

'Enjoying yourself?'

She tensed, hearing his book snap closed.

'It's heaven,' she lied, staring up at the rather jaded emulsion of the ceiling, trying not to sound as though something had been wrenched out of her gut just from imagining him with another woman, pretending to herself that she didn't care, so that with even more feigned brightness she was adding, 'The Victorians certainly had some things right.'

He made a cynical sound down his nostrils. 'Yes—if you had servants to lug in all the water—fill the darn thing for you.'

He had a point there, she thought, silently sympathising with their plight.

A light movement of her shoulder disturbed the water, revealing the proud taut curvature of her breasts. 'I could go along with that.'

He gave a soft, almost humourless chuckle. 'As a Victorian? I don't think so. Times were pretty harsh—especially for a woman. I'm afraid your talents as a make-up artist, dearest, would probably never have seen the light of day. In fact your hopes of any sort of a career would almost certainly have had to be shelved in favour of housekeeping. And you would have had all my children, Taylor, and liked it, with very little say in the matter.'

Damp tendrils framed her face as she studied him through the dark fringes of her lashes. Was he deliberately trying to provoke her into a response?

'There was always abstinence,' she reminded him pointedly, just in case he was, and saw one thick eyebrow arch in silent scepticism. 'Or would you,' she challenged, feeling antagonistic without any substantial reason, 'have exercised your legal right and beaten me if I'd said no?'

He seemed to consider this with some amusement for a moment. 'That would have been my prerogative.' His gaze, sliding over the caramel silk of her hair was suddenly burning with a dark intensity, conveying an overtly sensual message that matched the fevered heat beneath her skin. With slow and candid appreciation those febrile eyes roamed over the defiant tilt of her pointed chin, touching on her wet shoulders before coming to rest on her small and gleaming breasts. 'I don't think though,' he breathed, his voice suddenly low and husky, 'that any flaying of that tender flesh would ever have been necessary. I don't think there ever was or will be a time when either of us could have said—or could say—no. Which is why you're a fool if you imagine you can deny either of us, Taylor. Nature has a way of mocking us—and all the more for our efforts to contradict her, darling.'

As it had when she had got pregnant?

Unwillingly her mind skittered back to that time. Usually she would have been horrified at the thought of conceiving an unwanted child, at using no protection, but she had let him that night, too ensnared by the bitter-sweet aftermath of their quarrel to retain any measure of common sense. Getting pregnant was the last thing she had wanted, but Nature had had other ideas, opening her womb to his seed and forcing her—despite her worries, her resistance and the threat of breaking up—or perhaps, as he had suggested, because of all of those things—to accept that her body had selected this man as its mate and master, and that her genes would be melded with his, no matter what the cost.

Hurting, angry with herself, with him, and with the

forces of nature—or whatever had destined that she should be marooned here with him—she pushed herself up out of the water and grabbed the big fluffy towel from the arm of the chair just within her reach, foam cascading down over her glistening nakedness.

Keeping her back to him, quickly she proceeded to dry herself, her slim shoulders tense from the uncomfortable knowledge that he was watching her. She could sense his dark, almost tangible gaze travelling down over each vertebrae of her slender back to her tapering waist and tight neat bottom.

'My robe?' Unable to see it anywhere as she finished drying herself, she thrust her feet into a pair of open-toed mules and, with the damp towel draped around her, made a move towards the door, realising she must have left it upstairs.

'No you don't.' Jared's hard command stalled her. He was already getting to his feet. 'You'll catch your death of cold.'

He was back within a couple of minutes, striding over to warm the garment in front of the fire.

'Here.'

Discarding the towel, wishing he wasn't so close, Taylor slipped her arms into the robe he was holding out for her. The sleeves were still cold, but the body of it was nicely warm and she gave a delicious little shudder as she pulled it around her. However, on reaching for the belt, her fingers almost entwined with his and quickly she withdrew them, standing stock-still as his arms looped under hers so that he could tie the sash around her tiny waist.

He was looking over her shoulder, concentrating on what he was doing, while Taylor could hardly trust herself to breathe. She could hear his slow and steady breathing, feel its warmth against her hair, could envisage the thickness of those heavy lashes veiling his eyes. He smelled nice too, she noted, not daring to inhale too deeply that potent and very masculine scent that was all his own. But when a slight turn of her head brought her cheek into shocking contact with the rough texture of his jaw, something inside her snapped and all the resolve in the world couldn't hold back the sound that escaped her like a soft purr, or stop her from sinking back against him.

CHAPTER EIGHT

SHE felt his body stiffen, heard his breath catch as though he had been hit in the solar plexus, and she expected him to pull her round, devour her with the kisses she was craving from him to fulfil this aching need inside of her.

But instead his arms came across her body, holding her hard against him, every bone and muscle in that masculine frame tensed rigid, and yet, despite what he had said to her in the bath about not denying them both, exercising amazing control.

His lips were still against her cheek, and she could feel the tremors that shook his body, sense the battle he was having with himself not to give in to the hard desires that rode him. After a few moments though she felt him relax a little, loosen his embrace, leaving her aching for his arms as his firm warm hands slid sensuously over the silky sleeves of her robe.

'Tell me about Taylor Adams.' His voice was thick against the perfumed dampness of her hair.

She made a small, frustrated sound, born of desire. 'What do you want to know?'

'Who she is.' He was still caressing her, inhaling her clean fragrance.

She laughed then, a short breathy laugh. 'You know who I am!'

'No, I don't,' he countered heavily. 'Oh, I know that you're deep and mysterious, as well as being an incredibly sexy lady. I know you like it when I do this...' his hand moved slightly, making her groan from the exquisite friction of his thumb across the taut, tender peak of her breast

111

'…and this…' His other hand had slipped inside her robe and was moving down over the warm plane of her stomach, causing her to gasp and move restlessly against him when his seeking fingers cupped the moist heart of her femininity. 'But I want to understand you, Taylor. Understand the way you think. What you feel.'

She glanced down at the bath. The foam had all gone now, dispersed by the soap, leaving a cloudy film on the surface of the water.

'You lived with me for nearly two years!' she reminded him, mourning the loss of his hands when he suddenly stopped touching her.

'We were strangers,' he said succinctly, massaging her slender arms again. 'I'm ashamed to say it, but I didn't really know my wife.'

His voice, close to her ear, was incredibly arousing, stimulating every erogenous zone she possessed.

'Why are you so sure there's anything to understand?'

He pulled her round to face him at last. He looked flushed, she thought; aroused from touching her. Not at all immune under all that rigid self-discipline.

'Because the face you show the world isn't the real you. The real you's lost somewhere under a mask as thick and concealing as any you create for those stars and characters you work with. Because you're different in bed. In my bed you become a woman who isn't challenged or frozen out or scared by the strength of her own feelings.'

'I'm not scared—or frozen out,' she uttered in wounded defence. 'Whatever that's supposed to mean.'

'Then why won't you give us another chance? You like being with me. Even you can't deny that what we have is good—that *we're* good together.'

'No,' she agreed, with troubled lines scoring her forehead. 'But marriage is—was—different. And you'd start putting pressure on me to have children and I don't want that.'

His brows coming together, he studied her contemplatively for a moment. 'Children aren't the biggest issue in my life,' he said. 'What matters is you and me.'

Oh, if only she could believe that! 'That's not how you made me feel.'

Puzzlement etched the strong features as he looked at her askance. 'How did I make you feel?'

She couldn't meet his eyes levelly, keeping her gaze on the first fastened button of his shirt as she said dismally, 'As though I were just there because you needed a wife to provide you with the children you wanted.'

He laughed, not very humorously. 'My crazy little Taylor. I married you for *you*. OK, it's true I wanted children—a family—I still do—but not until my wife is happy about it—ready.'

'But I might never be. Don't you see...' The eyes she lifted to his held a plea for understanding, deepening the grove between the thick arches of his brows.

'Because of your career?'

Of course, he had thought her ambitious and single-minded, she reflected, remembering his mother.

'No,' she responded truthfully.

His eyes were clouded, questioning. 'Why then?'

'I don't know.'

'You're not making any sense,' he breathed. 'I've seen how you are with kids. How you were with Josh...'

'That's different,' she said. With little Josh she had no choice. She couldn't close herself off from Josh. And anyway, he was such an endearing little scamp, she didn't want to. 'It's different,' she reiterated. 'He isn't mine.' Nor was his happiness—his security—resting on her shoulders, or the whole frightening responsibility of his life. 'I don't feel secure enough to have a baby.'

'With me?' he pressed. 'Because of how it was between us?'

'Yes. No. I don't know,' she expressed, floundering. 'I
don't think I could ever feel secure with any man.'

How could she explain? It was much more complex and
deep-rooted than he could ever understand.

'If that was how you felt, shouldn't you have considered
that before you said ''yes'' to me?'

'Maybe, but I was…young…infatuated,' she said, picking her words, careful not to say, 'love', or anything that
might make him realise how deeply she still felt for him,
and therefore how little pressure it would take to sway her
into returning to him.

'Is that all it was? Is?' Something akin to pain seemed
to darken his eyes to inky black. 'Infatuation?'

'I don't know. No,' she uttered quickly, defending her
motives because he looked so…hurt, she couldn't bear it.

'It's solely because of Alicia, isn't it?' he said. 'Because
you knew I'd had an affair.' Visibly Taylor winced, and
heard him swear under his breath. 'Because some thoughtless, idle gossips couldn't keep their tongues from wagging
long enough not to make my newly-wedded bride aware of
it! To make you think I couldn't honour my own marriage
vows any more than I could honour anyone else's!'

'Look, it's my problem, all right?'

'No, this concerns us both.'

'Not when I don't want it to,' she said. 'And if you think
I should have considered things more before we were married, then so should you. You were the one who was in
such a hurry. You didn't give me time to think.'

'You make it sound as though I dragged you to the cer-
emony handcuffed. You were as keen as I was,' he reminded her.

Because she had been so in love with him that she had
been prepared to put her life—her welfare—in his hands—

and the welfare of her children—but that was before she had known she had a rival for his affections. She would hardly have had these fears and insecurities if she had been sure of him, would she? Or... Suddenly she found herself needing to ask herself the question. Would being faced with the prospect of a child under any circumstances have produced the same measure of anxiety? And if she hadn't lost her baby, what then? What if she *had* been right about him and the other woman, had tried to leave and he had refused to let her take his child away? Would she have stayed, borne the agony of his betrayal for her child's sake? Or would she have done the unthinkable? Simply...

She blocked out the thought before it could even take shape, unaware of the anguish that made a tight mask of her features. Her baby hadn't survived, so the question didn't arise, did it? she thought achingly.

'I hadn't realised that the thought of coming back to me was so abhorrent to you.'

The deep male voice sliced incisively through her thoughts as he abruptly released her.

Bereft, Taylor watched him cross the room and drop heavily down onto the settee where he sat glaring at the fire. The flames had died down but the basket was glowing with molten heat, a shimmering bed of embers, she noted distractedly.

'It isn't that...'

'Isn't it?' he rasped.

Unhappily, aching for his arms around her, she watched him lean forward to pick up a log, throw it into the embers with a sudden startling shower of sparks.

She felt desolate inside, but not as desolate as he looked, she noticed suddenly, wondering, as she had done on the fell that day, if there was the slimmest chance that all along she had been dreadfully wrong about him, just as she had been wrong in suggesting that infatuation was all she had felt for him, when love itself didn't begin to cover this hopeless need, desire and craving that filled every last corpuscle of her being.

Driven by that love and the desperate need to feel his tenderness again, she crossed over to stand in front of him and then, when he didn't look at her, knelt down between his parted knees.

'Let's not think about the past—or the future,' she whispered, making absent circles with her fingers over the soft corduroy just above his knee. 'Let's just take things as they come, all right?'

'As they come?' He leaned forward and rested his hands on her shoulders, looking down into her eyes from the dark, fathomless pools of his own.

'Without any rush.' Her voice was a whisper from the depth of wanting that was flooding through her, her hands lifting to the abrasive and exciting texture of his skin just below his cheeks.

'No pressure.' His lips on hers were gentle, tentatively probing. 'OK.' The syllables came as a trembling murmur against her mouth. 'If that's what you want.'

What she wanted…!

Suddenly what she wanted was to show him how much she loved him, and no matter what happened tomorrow, the next day, or in the future, tonight he was hers, she reminded herself, and she intended to make it a night that he would always remember.

She had never taken the initiative with him so completely before, but now she gently pressed him back against the settee and while the fire leaped and danced with renewed vigour, she set out to please him, delighting in his groans of ecstasy, the knowledge that this hard-headed, brilliant man was reduced to such sensual enslavement through the sheer power of her femininity. And a little later, when he could endure no more of such exquisite torment, he left her, though merely to fetch something to protect her from any clearly unwanted pregnancy.

Taking the initiative again, she straddled him, pleased by his deep groan of appreciation that she was still enjoying taking the lead. But the reality of his filling her again was too unbearably exquisite and with a gasp of shuddering ecstasy, she lost control.

Which was when he took over, she realised, welcoming it as he snatched the clasp from her hair and, sinking his fingers into the thick caramel swathe, pulled her down to lock his mouth with hers, joining her with him in a rapturous togetherness of mind, body and soul.

The following morning she awoke in the big bed in the master bedroom, feeling pleasingly warm and, hearing the sound of water running in the bathroom, guessed that Jared was taking a shower.

A *shower*!

Realising that that could only mean that the power had come back on, she slipped naked out of bed and into her robe, revelling in the luxury of modern-day central heating, though the warmth she was feeling inside had nothing to do with the heat in the room.

She had spent a long, luxurious night in what could only be described as paradise, she reflected happily, thinking of the passion and tenderness they had shared in equal measure as she padded barefoot into the bathroom, her heart leaping like some crazy schoolgirl's when she saw Jared's big bronzed body through the steam in the cubicle, soapy and gleaming with shower gel.

'Good morning. Come to join me?' he drawled, wiping steam from the glass.

'You wish!' she laughed rather breathlessly, thinking of those exciting showers they had taken together in the early days of their marriage, thinking also of the bath he had

prepared for her the previous day and how, tired and fulfilled by his lovemaking afterwards, she had slept so
deeply, lying there on the settee, that when she had woken
it was to find the tub gone as if spirited away by magic.
'After all your time and energy getting a bath for me yesterday!' she mocked, teasing him, because secretly it had
been wonderful. 'Had I known the power was coming back
on I would have waited a few more hours and just taken a
shower!'

'Oh, would you?' came the deep reply through the gush
of the water. 'Be a good girl and pass me that towel, will
you?' A jerk of his chin indicated the fluffy white bath
sheet on the heated rail behind her but, as she was handing
it to him, too late she realised what his intention was when
strong wet fingers caught her wrist, and with a determined,
'You still can!' he was yanking her in beside him under
the powerful jets.

'No,' she shrieked, unprepared for the sudden soaking.
'I've still got my robe on!'

She was grappling for her balance, trying to see through
her wet hair, meeting the warm sensuality of wet masculine
flesh and catching his deep, sexy laugh as he told her,
'Well, we'll soon change that!'

The next minute she was as naked as he was, her drip-
ping robe thrown carelessly over the cubicle door, her lips
and hands as eager for him as those already using their
mind-blowing skill on her sensitised body, desire swallowing them both up with this insatiable need for each other
that was as fundamental and untamed as the frozen landscape beyond the window.

The freeze-up continued throughout the week.

'If this weather persists and I can't get home, I shan't be
able to go on location next Tuesday,' Taylor worried one
evening as the weekend drew ever nearer, concerned for

her job and the three-week assignment about which she had already told him. It was to be a mythological documentary set in Greece.

'In that case it will be Aphrodite's loss and my gain,' Jared remarked, clearly approving as he looked up with a meaningful smile from the book he was reading.

'Yes, and wouldn't that just please you?' Taylor pretended to object, flushing just from imagining being snowed up here like this with him indefinitely. Even just sitting, quietly reading, as they were now, filled her with such pleasurable contentment that she felt she wouldn't have cared if they never got back to London.

Since the night Jared had promised not to put any more pressure on her, he had kept to his word, and she had never felt happier with him, she decided, since the time when, newly married, they had come here first.

Sometimes, she dared to contemplate that she could even be happier now, although she kept such thoughts pretty much to herself. Any hint of how she was feeling and she was sure Jared would start metaphorically twisting her arm to resume their old life again, and she didn't want anything to wreck the very fragile happiness she seemed to have found with him in this frozen wilderness.

That afternoon, with a crazy lightness of heart, she made a snowman in the front garden, defending her endeavours when Jared came out and teased her mercilessly about it.

'My word, you must be bored! And I thought I was keeping you suitably occupied,' he mocked.

'Obviously not,' Taylor laughed, shaping her snowman, putting on an artistic show of lovingly finishing it off. 'You're just jealous.'

'Of course I am,' he remarked, absently twirling the woollen hat he had been wearing that day on the toboggan. 'I'm jealous of anything that takes you away from me. Anyway, I thought eyes were round,' he commented, grimacing at the two multi-sided silver coins she was slotting in above a stubby stick of a nose. 'I know eyes have corners, but *seven*!'

'I couldn't find anything else. Besides,' Taylor went on, her cheeks glowing as much from her awareness of Jared's vibrant presence as from working in the clean, cold air. 'These are sharp eyes.'

'Oh, very droll!' he laughed, his breath rising on a warm cloud. 'What are they going to do? Watch all we do?' His mouth took on a sensually inspired curve. 'That should keep him entertained.'

'You…!' Swiftly, Taylor scooped up a handful of snow, and was disappointed when he sidestepped, dodging the ball as she tried to pelt him with it. 'It's you he's going to be watching!'

'Want to bet?' With a couple of strides forward he was stretching the hat he had brought out over her snowman's head, tugging it down over its 'eyes'. 'That takes care of that! Now…' He was already straightening with a huge handful of compressed snow and, with a shriek, Taylor darted away only to underestimate how cleverly he would gauge her movements and paid for it with a very accurate and retaliatory pelt on her backside.

'That's not fair!' she pretended to protest, rubbing the back of her wet jeans. She could see him laughing and found it difficult keeping a straight face as he strode over to her. 'You can hit harder than I can.'

'You know what they say about people who live in glass houses.'

'"Shouldn't throw stones"? I know.' She laughed up at him provocatively now. 'But I like living dangerously.'

'In that case you're in for one hell of a *smashing* time.'

'You…!' Flushing from his sensual pun, she pushed at him hard, wondering why they had never enjoyed such a childlike sense of playfulness together before; loving every second she shared with him like this.

Amusement still crinkled the corners of his eyes as he caught her, pulling her against him, melting her insides as his cool, firm mouth took gentle possession of hers.

Desire, never far away, rose up in her as the skylarks that nested there in spring would rise high above the valley, and she murmured her longing, her need, everything that encompassed her deepening love for this man. And she knew in that moment as he lifted his head to look at her, and she saw the depth of emotion in his eyes, that if he pressed her again to go back to him she would have no choice but to agree to it, because after all this and the memories they had created here this week, life would be too unbearable without him.

During the next couple of days the skies turned grey, bringing with them a slight rise in temperature so that by Saturday, with the snow already beginning to thaw, their lane was passable to cautious traffic.

'All the main roads are clear,' Taylor, having just heard the travel news on the radio, told Jared as he brought her breakfast in bed that morning. South of the Midlands, it seemed, they'd had hardly any snow at all. 'So at least we can get back today without any hassle.'

Originally, thinking she would be on her own in Cumbria, she hadn't intended to stay away all week. Therefore, she was surprised when, now the weekend had arrived, Jared suddenly said, 'Let's go home tomorrow.'

'That will give me one day to prepare for Greece! Monday,' she pointed out laughingly. But the thought of spending an extra day with him, without any cares or pressures was tempting, and already her brain was working out if it could possibly be achieved.

'Stay,' Jared reiterated on a soft command as he set the

tray with the delicious smelling breakfast he had cooked for her down in front of her on the duvet.

So she did, waking on Sunday morning to find that, during the night the temperature had lifted considerably and the thaw had well and truly set in.

Patches of grassy moorland, which for days had lain under a thick covering of snow, were showing green again, while across the patchwork fields in the valley, the russet of a clump of beech trees was already reflected in the emerging colours on the lower slopes of the fells that faced the sun.

It wouldn't matter that they were going home today, Taylor thought, or that within the next couple of days she would be rushing off to another assignment. They had built something together here—something more than just a snowman, she thought wryly, looking down on her carefully sculpted efforts which were now just a shapeless melting pillar with a woolly hat stuck on top. What they had created here was something special and precious, she decided, and though she didn't feel entirely ready yet to commit herself to resuming their old life together, she felt surer of her own feelings and of Jared.

She just wished she wasn't going away. Not now. Not just when things were beginning to look so promising for them. But though the time might drag without him, she knew that what they had shared up here together would see her through the hectic days and lonely nights while she was on location, that her love and desire and the mounting anticipation and excitement of seeing him again would keep her going until she returned home.

She did think about asking him out to join her for a few days if he could spare the time from making multi-million-pound decisions and negotiating important deals or, at the very least, to fly out for a couple of long weekends, although she dismissed that idea, not wanting to appear too keen, deciding to leave it to him to make the suggestion himself, as she felt sure he would.

'You were so lucky, being brought up here,' she murmured to him when they were enjoying one last walk after breakfast and had just reached the top of the slope where he had had her screaming on that crazy toboggan ride. It seemed so distant now—so distant in terms of how far they seemed to have come over the past week, she might have dreamt it, Taylor decided with a wistful smile. 'When you asked me to come here to sort out my things, I thought it was because you were planning on selling the house,' she admitted, and then, as the thought took hold, 'You won't, will you?' she asked, turning anxious green eyes his way.

'I've made no plans to,' he drawled, without looking at her, his superbly masculine profile never failing—as it ever had done—to take her breath away. She was standing beside him, absorbing the stunning beauty of the landscape, silently marvelling at the sheer scale of the mountains, of the plunging valley with its lush meadows and crystal-clear rivers, seeing everything through his eyes—the eyes of the man she loved. 'If I hadn't had this place, I'd hardly have spent such a wonderful week with such a thrilling and delightful captive, would I?' he commented, his mouth twitching as he turned to her now.

'Captive?' she queried lightly, challenging his rather macho remark, her tilted head gleaming like smooth bronze in the sun. 'My jailer was the snow. Not you.'

He dipped his head in subtle acknowledgement. 'And now the thaw's set in.'

What was he saying? she wondered, her pulse quickening from those darkly scrutinising eyes, from the hidden meaning she sensed behind his casual remark. Was he suggesting she was his again now? That she would move back into his apartment, as quickly and as eagerly as she had stepped back into his bed? Twin shafts of panic and excitement arrowed through her. She wasn't sure she was ready for that. Not yet!

'Race you back!' she prompted, knowing it would be obvious to him that she was evading the issue, but she didn't care. She was already running away from him, down the slope.

Half an hour later, with Jared loading up the cars, she was just tidying up the sitting room, when the telephone rang.

CHAPTER NINE

'TAYLOR?' Steven Shaunessy's voice was hesitant, strung with surprise.

'Steven,' she acknowledged, her smile evident in those two syllables. 'What can I do for you?'

'I—I didn't realise the two of you were back together.'

He sounded embarrassed, Taylor thought, and wondered what to say. Were they? Back together? The prospect scared as much as it excited her.

Feeling rather awkward, she gave a pointless little shrug and without committing herself said, 'Well...you never know.'

'I'm sorry to ring you up there,' he expressed even more hesitantly. 'But I've been trying to get hold of Jared since yesterday. Could I...um...speak to him...if he's there?'

He sounded worried, Taylor decided, wondering what crisis must have happened within the company while its kingpin had been snowed up in the Lakes.

'I'll get him,' she offered, just as Jared came through the door.

'It's for you,' she told him when he jerked his chin in silent query as to who was telephoning. 'Steve.' And with her hand over the mouthpiece, she whispered, 'He sounds a bit worried.'

He received this information with the slightest tug of his mouth, the simple wink he gave her making her stomach flip as did the casual brush of his hand against hers as he took the phone from her.

Moving across to the mantelpiece, she stopped, duster

poised in hand when she heard his deeply rasped, 'Oh, dear, no!'

Glancing at him over her shoulder, she noticed that his face had gone quite pale and his skin appeared to be drawn tightly over his cheekbones.

For a split second his eyes clashed with hers, but he seemed to look right through her before turning purposefully away.

'Did you say where I was?' There was a pause while Taylor tried to assess the emotions lacing the deep masculine tones. What was it that was making him sound so concerned? So uncharacteristically worried?

Pale grey dust lined the mantelpiece from the fires they had lit over the past week and when she removed the candlesticks with the intention of returning them to the kitchen, where she had found them, there were two dark circles where they had been standing.

Like oases in a grey-white desert, she thought whimsically. Representative of her and Jared, alone here together in the snow.

Dusting the old clock in the centre of the mantelpiece, her back locked rigid when she heard him whisper almost inaudibly, 'Not now.'

Quickly she looked round, but he still had his back to her. With the phone held tightly to his ear, his head was bowed as though for added privacy. The knuckles of the hand splayed across the back of one hip were white with tension, and the rise and fall of his upper torso beneath the chunky sweater suggested that he was breathing more heavily than usual.

'All right. *All right.*' He exhaled those last two words as if he had just been forced to make a life-changing decision. 'We were leaving today anyway. I'll be back within a few hours.'

'What is it?' Taylor asked, frowning as he returned the

phone to its rest with quiet, almost measured precision and stood, with his back to her, both hands in his pockets, staring out of the window. 'What's wrong?'

He turned around then, releasing another laboured breath.

'It's Alicia,' he said, and Taylor's heart sank. 'Her husband had a heart attack three weeks ago. It was fatal. She's coming over to see me. Steve said she's already on her way.'

'What?' She couldn't believe she was hearing correctly. 'Why?' she demanded to know, but it was more like an injured cry. 'Why would she want to see you?' Yet she knew the answer even before he responded.

'I can only surmise.'

'Yes. Can't we all!'

'Taylor, for heaven's sake—'

'You're not going to see her?' She couldn't believe that he was even considering it—not after the past few days that they had spent together.

'What do you expect me to do? Pick up the phone and send her packing on the first plane back? Or perhaps you think my secretary should do it for me. Would that be a more suitable course of action for you?'

She shook her head, but in exasperation rather than negation. 'I just don't see why you think you're even obligated to do as she's suggesting, that's all.'

'Because I've known her a long time and she isn't coming from just down the road.' Tensely, he was massaging his neck with the palm of his hand. 'She's coming from Philadelphia. Therefore common courtesy wouldn't allow me to do anything else.'

'Apart from that—you want to.' She could see it in his eyes. She could recognise anguish when she saw it; see the battle he was having with himself between what was right and what his long-buried love for the other woman was driving him to do. 'You really want to see her, don't you? Well, if you do, don't expect me to calmly wait around!'

As she went to flounce away, he caught her roughly to face him, the hands gripping her upper arms bruising her tender flesh. 'For heaven's sake! Don't be so unreasonable.'

'Unreasonable!' Forcibly she shrugged out of his grasp. 'My husband's mistress has lost hers and she's coming over to claim mine! Great!' With one expressive gesture she swiped her duster over the mantelpiece, so that the round dark rings where the candlesticks had stood disappeared like mirages in the sand.

Like the past week had been, she thought bitterly. Just an illusion of happiness. The product of a lovesick, over-optimistic mind!

'There's no need for this to affect us,' she heard him state decisively behind her.

'Isn't there?' She didn't look at him, just went on dusting the shelf, picking up ornaments, putting them down again, her movements agitated, her insides in turmoil.

'Taylor, look at me.'

She didn't want to, but the imperativeness of his tone wasn't to be totally ignored.

'No, look at me,' he commanded gently when she met him halfway by turning round but kept her eyes fixed firmly on the soft dark leather of his moccasins. 'Come on,' he pressed softly. 'I don't bite.'

Reluctantly, she let her gaze travel along the solid length of his body, reluctantly remembering how smooth and warm it would feel, rippling with strength beneath those thick and coarse casual clothes.

'Do you really think my seeing Alicia poses a threat to us? After all we've done—enjoyed together—here—over the past week?'

If only she could believe it! she thought achingly, realising that her doubt must have conveyed itself to him when she didn't answer, because in a voice as smooth as melting chocolate, he said, 'Come here.'

This time she obeyed instantly, drawn by the power of his will and of her love for him into the warm, inviting circle of his arms.

His lips on hers were tender, while hers were urgent and searching, willing him to deepen his kiss with a desperation born out of her uncertainties and fears.

'This isn't a lover's parting,' he murmured against her mouth, the rapidity of his breathing evidence that he hadn't wanted to stop any more than she did. But, lifting his head, he held her away from him, saying only, 'Trust me.'

For a long moment his gaze tugged over her. As though, Taylor thought, in spite of what he had just said, he was trying to imprint every last detail of her on his consciousness, from the sleek but simple style of her hair to her fine, but certainly not exquisite features, and her rather too willowy figure.

'All it means is that we won't see each other tonight,' he told her, 'which we probably wouldn't have done anyway. But I'll...sort things out this evening and we'll make a date for tomorrow night, I promise.'

She wished she could have felt more reassured as he went back out to finish whatever he had been doing outside.

With very little time to pack for three weeks on location, Taylor started on the job almost as soon as she arrived back at the flat.

No sooner had she begun than the ringing of her doorbell announced company in the shape of Charity.

'We were so worried about you,' her landlady expressed, coming in with a carrier bag, which she brought through into the kitchen. 'The weather was horrible here, but nothing like you had it in the North. You must have been snowed in, surely? How on earth did you manage?'

'It wasn't so bad.' Gratefully, Taylor took the things Charity always insisted on supplying when she had been away. There was bread and milk and a few freshly prepared salad ingredients, she noted, putting the milk in the fridge, trying to sound casual as she tagged on, 'Jared came up for a few days.'

One auburn eyebrow shot up to meet the crinkled mane of equally auburn hair. 'Really?' There was more than a little intrigue woven into that one word.

'There were things we needed to sort out.' Aiming for equilibrium, Taylor went over to fetch her purse from the worktop to pay Charity for the groceries.

'I see.'

No you don't, Taylor thought, dropping coins back into her purse when Charity waved them aside. Because how could she explain to her friend that the husband she had spent the last impassioned week with was probably right now in the company of some other woman; a woman whose lover he had once been and who was now entirely free to resume their relationship if that was what he wanted?

'I don't know...you're so cool,' Charity laughed. 'If I hadn't married the most wonderful man on earth, there's nothing I would have liked better than to be snowed up with a man like Jared! Don't tell me it wasn't...interesting.'

'I won't,' Taylor parried. Because it had been heaven! Heaven, that was, until that phone call from Steve Shaunessy, telling him that Alicia was on her way over. After that, however, reassuring though Jared had tried to be, he had also been preoccupied and he certainly hadn't wasted any more time in coming home!

He had kept her in his sights all the way down the motorway, though once or twice, piqued by his lack of understanding about the way she was feeling, she had done her level best to lose him, but there he had been, on her tail again, every time she thought she had. Then, with a sudden aggressive flash of his lights, as they had approached the slip-road for his junction, he had pulled out and smoothly and swiftly overtaken her, mocking her earlier attempts to lose him with more power, more nerve, just more all-round experience, she had thought resentfully, watching the dark saloon shooting off along the outside lane, carrying him back to his luxurious apartment, his own life, and to another woman.

'Do you know what I think?' Charity said, preparing to return to the hectic domesticity downstairs. 'I think you want him back, but you're too scared to admit it.'

Yes she was scared, Taylor thought, realising that her landlady had hit the nail squarely on the head. Scared of committing herself. Scared of loving him too much. Scared that he wouldn't come back.

Which was totally unjustified, the voice of reason tried to reassure her. Because surely he wouldn't have followed her to Cumbria, put pressure on her to go back to him, and loved her with such exquisite consideration for her pleasure if he didn't feel anything for her—would he?

OK. So perhaps he had wanted them both to pick up where they had left off, the voice of doubt chipped in over her reasoning. But supposing he saw Alicia and realised that he was still in love with her; that it was *her* he would rather be with after all? It wasn't uncommon for a man to want one woman, and to truly love another. And supposing she tried to persuade him...

Here Taylor pulled up her runaway thoughts, glad that she didn't have time to dwell too deeply on what might be happening between her husband and the lovely American widow. Because she would be lovely—Taylor was certain of it, although she had never seen a photograph of the woman, or ever enquired of Jared what she was like. That she had been a constant threat to—and throughout—her marriage had been knowledge enough.

But there were other things to think about, she told herself firmly, like putting the washer-dryer on to launder the clothes she had brought back from Cumbria, washing her hair and finishing most of her packing, determined as she was that when she did see Jared the following evening, they could enjoy quality time together before she went off for three weeks, without her having a lot of unnecessary jobs to do.

She was feeling well and truly keyed up when she arrived at the studios the next day, jumping whenever the telephone rang, expecting it to be him. She had been half hoping that he would ring last night before she went to bed, although perhaps he hadn't seen the woman yet, Taylor consoled herself and didn't want to telephone until he had. It couldn't be an entirely pleasant task for him, she thought, having to tell someone who thought they had some claim on you that they didn't. So perhaps he was in the same state of nervous anticipation as she was, she reasoned, wishing she were with him, planning, as soon as she had a minute to herself, the menu for a special dinner for them both that night.

She was just considering where to buy the Cointreau to pour over the fresh pineapple and ginger ice cream she had settled on for dessert when her mobile phone rang.

'Taylor?'

Relief flooded through her just from hearing his deep voice. Her heart was pumping like a lovesick teenager's. 'Yes.' It was an eager, breathless response. But the silence that followed was just that little bit too long. 'Jared?'

'Taylor…' Tension coiled her insides from the thread of hesitancy in his voice. She caught the sound of a deeply indrawn breath. 'I'm afraid you aren't going to like this— but I'm going to have to cancel tonight.'

No!

'W-what do you mean?' He couldn't be saying this. He

couldn't! 'What do you mean—you're going to have to cancel?' Fear lined her forehead and the sudden pains in her stomach made her want to double up. He had to work. That was it. He was cancelling because of the pressures of his job.

'Look, I'm sorry. I wouldn't have planned this for the world.'

'Planned what?' What was he talking about? 'Have you seen Alicia?'

'Yes, I have, and she's in a pretty bad state.'

'She's in—' What did he expect? For the woman to shower them with her blessings? 'And how the hell am I supposed to feel? I'm going away tomorrow. I'm not going to be back for three weeks—or had you forgotten that?'

'No, I hadn't forgotten.'

'So what are you planning to do? Hold her hand until she's feeling better? Couldn't she take being told that you prefer your wife!'

'Taylor...'

'Or is she feeling so bad because suddenly she's all alone in the world?'

'Neither.'

'Putting on a façade of sorrowing widowhood because she can't take being rejected by somebody else's husband?' And as something clicked in her brain, uncertainly she asked, 'You *have* told her...haven't you?'

'No,' he said decisively. 'I haven't.'

'You haven't? What do you mean you haven't? You promised!' Suddenly she could hear the high ring of her mother's voice, echoing down through the years. 'You said it was over! You said—'

'Taylor, I'm not going to stand here reiterating everything I'm supposed to have said when you're too bull-headed even to listen.' He was speaking in a lowered voice, as though someone else might be listening; as though someone was there, she thought all of a sudden. 'The fact is Alicia's ill. She has food poisoning—she thinks from something she ate on the plane—but she isn't well enough to be left on her own in a hotel. She isn't well enough to be left on her own—period. I've moved her into the apartment.'

'You what?' She couldn't believe he was saying this—couldn't convince herself that it wasn't all an excuse because he hadn't yet worked out how to tell her that, despite the glorious and intimate week they had just shared together, it was the other woman he still wanted. 'Until when?' she challenged bitterly.

'How the hell do I know?' He sounded irritable—impatient. 'Until she's better. And don't ask me when that will be, because I don't know. I thought at the very least you'd try to understand. *It isn't possible for me to leave her.*' He breathed every word with deliberate emphasis. 'If you refuse to, that's up to you.'

'Oh, I understand,' she murmured painfully. He was prepared to let his wife fly off to Greece for three weeks without even saying goodbye, and all because another woman who had flown over to see him—the woman he'd kept insisting he had finished with a long time ago—had a stomach-ache! He couldn't have conveyed a clearer message if he had tried.

'Taylor, don't make this more difficult.' He exhaled heavily as though he were weary of the whole conversation—as though he wished he could wind it up. Perhaps he did, she thought, achingly. 'She's alone in a foreign country. She's ill and she doesn't know a soul. Can't you see I don't have any choice?'

'Yes, I can see clearly.' She couldn't help the sarcasm. It was all that was keeping her from falling apart. Because surely if Alicia really was unwell, couldn't he have found *someone* to look after her? But, no. He just wanted to be with her and he was going to any length he thought fit to make it possible!

'No, you don't. You don't see anything,' he returned, more harshly now. 'You're so visually impaired you couldn't see the moon through a telescope! The truth is you're already so sure about my infidelity with Alicia, there's absolutely no point in my denying it, is there?'

What was he saying?

'You'll never let this thing go until you've screwed an admission out of me, because that's the only scenario that warped little brain of yours can accept!'

'That's not true!' she defended herself, wondering why he was trying to make it seem as though it was all her fault; that she was wrong in wanting her husband to be with her and not some other woman the night before she went away; that she actually wanted to hear him say he was having an affair. 'I think any woman in her right mind would feel exactly the same way as I do. And if you expect me to believe she's so ill you can't drag yourself away from her to be with me, then there's something radically wrong.'

'It's all I can come up with, Taylor. Take it or leave it.'

She hadn't even realised she had slammed down the phone until it was too late.

CHAPTER TEN

'THAT,' said Craig, handing Taylor a still from one of their recent productions, 'just shows what a brilliant make-up artist you are.'

Shielding her eyes from the bright Mediterranean sunshine, Taylor pulled a wry face at the ostensibly flawless complexion of the woman in the photograph, whose scar left by a recent boating accident appeared to have been totally obliterated.

'It could be more a case of clever lighting,' she responded carelessly, deflecting the praise to accommodate Craig's talents. 'That and some skilled photography.' She had to say that because even though she wasn't Paul Salisbury's biggest fan, there was no getting away from the fact that he was one of the best at his job in the business. Apart from which he was standing by the rocks, just a few metres away, blond hair as sun-washed as the white houses on the hills behind him, twisting a new lens onto his camera.

'Rare praise indeed, coming from the Ice Maiden,' he commented above the gentle wash of the waves over the shingle. 'Who knows? Perhaps she found someone to melt that heart of hers up there in Cumbria last week. Unless she saw enough ice and snow to realise what a turn-off it can be.'

'Take no notice of him,' Craig said gently as the other man moved off across the beach to shoot the first take of a Lancashire-bred Aphrodite rising from the sea. And, with a jerk of his chin towards the photograph she had just handed back to him, 'The credit's still all yours.'

'Thanks.' Her smile was soft and sad. Well that was what she was good at, she thought—disguising scars.

She hadn't told anyone—even Charity—about that telephone conversation she had had with Jared the day before she had left, and the woman hadn't pressed her any further with regard to her relationship with him, for which Taylor was immensely grateful. She didn't think she could have spoken about him without getting emotional—giving herself away as to how deeply she was hurting inside.

Following that conversation with Jared, which she had ended by slamming down the phone, she had been unbearably hurt and angry. But gradually, as day turned into evening, and the evening into a miserable, sleepless night, she had started wondering if she hadn't been rather unreasonable in not listening to him.

Perhaps Alicia really was ill and he had merely been considering another fellow human being who couldn't look after herself. Perhaps she should have been more understanding as he had expected her to be; a little less ready to think the worst. But, the thing was, she hadn't been sure and that was what had tortured her the most.

By the morning, however, longing to hear from him, prepared to listen—to give him the benefit of the doubt, frustrated by having to go away, she had swallowed her pride and telephoned the apartment, her heart beating like crazy as she waited for him to pick up the phone. But it had just rung and rung, without even the answering machine kicking in, and all Taylor's resolve to be reasonable—her self-chastisement over only thinking of herself—just crumbled away to nothing. He had said he couldn't possibly leave the woman. So why wasn't he there to answer the phone if he couldn't go anywhere? And why wasn't the answering machine on as it always used to be when he wasn't at home—or was unable to take his calls. Why hadn't he had them diverted to his mobile phone?

The questions had gone round and round her brain until the only realistic answer she could come up with was that he had gone out and simply forgotten. And what would make him do a thing like that? Nothing, she had decided wretchedly, unless he was so overwhelmed by the company he was keeping, it had driven everything else from his mind! In which case it had all been lies—just an excuse, she thought, tortured—when he had said he was unable to see her.

Racked by grief, anger and bitter recriminations, she had flown here to Greece with the rest of the team that day, with mental images of her husband and this unknown woman, off somewhere enjoying themselves together, tearing her apart.

That was ten days ago and she hadn't heard a word from him. What made it worse was that he could easily have contacted her if he had wanted to. But the thing that hurt most was that he could have set out to seduce her back into his bed, convincing her he wanted their marriage to continue, and after driving her delirious with his lovemaking— taking advantage of her hopeless love for him, he could just walk away from her afterwards as though nothing had happened; trade it all for the pleasure in another woman's arms.

The only redeeming factor, she decided now—absently watching Craig disappear into one of the mobile units set up for the filming—was that Jared didn't know just how much she loved him.

So many times the previous week, during their moments of blind, soul-consuming passion, the words had nearly tumbled from her lips, but something had always held her back, and she was glad now that it had. While he thought she was still unsure of her feelings for him, at least she could hold on to some dignity. But if he had known for certain how crazy she was about him… She couldn't even contemplate the humiliation of his knowing that.

No, she told herself with a firmness that nevertheless did nothing to make her feel any better. She had done the right thing in not letting her true feelings for him be known.

But now another worry that had been niggling away at her for days—and at the very heart of all her other worries—surfaced, that of whether or not she might be pregnant.

Her period was already late, probably—she was determined to convince herself—because of all the emotional upheaval, before, during and since those reckless days snowed up in Cumbria with Jared. Oh, he had been very careful after that first time, knowing how adversely she viewed becoming pregnant. But it was the folly of their first night together that was giving rise to her concern.

She thought about buying a pregnancy testing kit, but kept putting it off and knew that it was because she was afraid. While she didn't know, it still wasn't real and she wanted to keep it that way.

She didn't know how she got through the next few days, and was grateful that her work kept her busy. Turning high-spirited, sometimes temperamental actors into Greek gods and goddesses didn't stop her from thinking about Jared, but at least it kept her from dwelling too much on what might have resulted from her stupidly irresponsible behaviour with him. It was at night, however, when she couldn't sleep, that the disturbing thoughts crowded in.

What would he do if she went back home and told him she had conceived up there in Cumbria? To a man like Jared wouldn't honour and duty mean everything? Even though he was in love with someone else, he would probably try to insist on making their marriage work, she thought unhappily. But could she cope with that, knowing that in time he would probably resent her? Would she even tell him? Oh, heaven! How could she have got herself into such a fix!

A couple of days later she awoke with a fuzzy head, feeling bloated and generally fatigued and had to virtually drag herself out of the small hotel she was sharing with the others to get to the set.

By mid-morning the fuzziness had turned into a full-blown headache, and grabbing a couple of painkillers from her handbag she tripped across to one of the mobile units where, to her unexpected surprise and disbelief, she discovered she wasn't pregnant after all.

Her first feeling was of sublime relief. Weakened by it, and by a sudden swift rush of other, unexpected emotions, she couldn't go anywhere for a moment, closing her eyes as her head dropped forward against the door of the cubicle.

So overwhelming were the emotions that for a second she couldn't breathe, but then with one shuddering gasp she was giving in to them, her sobs coming loudly and uncontrollably.

Surely, she thought, she hadn't wanted his baby! She hadn't wanted a careless accident to rob her of any choice, to determine her life? Did she love him so much that she could sacrifice all the promises she had made to herself—all her resolve—for a situation against which she had always steeled herself? What had she been hoping? That it would make Jared come back to her? Or at the very least bind him to her in the age-old way women had been binding their men to them for centuries, because the prospect of never seeing him again was far too painful to comprehend?

She emerged from the unit looking no more than a little pale, her blotchy face washed and skilfully touched up from the set's effective *maquillage*, her red and puffy eyes concealed behind dark glasses so that no one could see that she had been crying.

Craig did, however, send a curious glance in her direction as he stepped down from the other unit with a mug of coffee in his hand, while during the afternoon even Paul seemed to sense that she wasn't feeling her best, refraining from any of his customary snipes at her. And, even though her mind was elsewhere, she was conscious of the whole film crew treading more delicately than usual around her. Everyone, it seemed, sensed there was something wrong, even if no one asked what it was, and Taylor was grateful for once for the persona of aloofness she had unintentionally created for herself that protected her from any intrusion into her privacy.

Glad though she had been to get away, she was even more grateful when the filming was over and she could return home. Which only seemed to emphasise the futility of trying to escape from herself! she thought, arriving back at the flat on a dull, damp Wednesday afternoon three weeks later, to find a note from Charity on the kitchen worktop under the little cherry loaf cake she had made for her.

'Hope you managed to get some sun. Garage called to say your car was ready.'

Frowning, Taylor grabbed her mobile phone and wandered through the flat, opening windows.

She hadn't even noticed her car wasn't parked outside! she realised, giving herself a mental shake for the state into which she was allowing herself to sink, wondering, as she tapped out the digits of the number scribbled on the note, if Charity had seen the damage to the wing and decided to book the car in for repair while she was away.

It wasn't normally the sort of thing her friend would do without telling her though, even if she did hold the spare key, Taylor thought, puzzled, going through to the bedroom and opening the window in there just as she was connected.

'You said my car was ready,' she told the owner of the

rather surly male voice at the other end of the line, giving him her name. 'Did Mrs Lucas bring it in?'

She waited, heard the shuffle of papers, then the unfriendly voice mechanically quoting the model of her car and registration number. 'Your husband brought it in,' he stated uninterestedly.

Jared? Excitement leaped like a spirited, uncontrolled filly inside of her.

'My husband?' How could he? she thought, baffled, then realised that he must have got hold of the key from Charity.

'As I said, it's ready for collection,' the man's voice broke in, then the connection at the other end was cut.

Suddenly her foolish excitement gave way to a suspicious hurt. Why was he doing this? she wondered, suspecting his motives. To show her he was still in control? That still being her husband gave him certain privileges—some sort of claim over her life? Or was he merely trying to force her into making contact with him? And if so, why?

Her blood began to race as she dared to wonder if she had been unjustifiably hasty in condemning him; if his reasons for cancelling their last evening together had been as well-founded as he had tried to make her believe. In which case, she had treated him abominably, she thought, aching, in spite of all the resolutions she had made while she had been away, to hear from him again.

But he didn't contact you, did he? Even as her fingers itched to pick out his number, more doubts were crowding in. Like, why hadn't he called her? Was it because he had been too busy entertaining Alicia? And had he now decided he preferred what he had with her, Taylor, instead? Or was he imagining he could have the best of both worlds now that she was back, knowing that she—sensually enslaved fool that she was—was bound to him, heart, mind and body, unable ever to resist that lethal magnetism of his?

Well, whatever, he would have to have enlisted Charity's

help, Taylor realised, having once more convinced herself of the worst, angry to think that he had been able to charm her friend into simply handing over her car keys to him. Oh, why couldn't he leave her alone!

Determined that such manipulation was going to backfire on him, Taylor decided that she wasn't going to instantly ring him, if that was what he was hoping. She'd pick up her car and speak to him some other time—possibly over the weekend.

It only occurred to her then, however, that she didn't have a clue as to the name of the garage, or where it was; that she had been so flummoxed by Jared's actions, she hadn't even thought to ask, and the attitude of the man to whom she had spoken over the phone wasn't exactly an open invitation to her ringing back.

Still there was nothing else she could do, she thought with a grimace, pressing the *Redial* button, but the only response to her call this time was a continuous ringing tone.

A glance at her watch showed that it was just after five-thirty, which probably meant that the office was closed even if the body repair shop was still open she thought, silencing her phone with an exasperated sigh.

Agitatedly, she nibbled at a nail. She could ring again in the morning, she deliberated, get a cab over to wherever it was. She didn't have anything urgent on in the morning, so no one would mind her taking an hour or so off.

She didn't like the idea of not even knowing where the car was, however, and a small rush of adrenalin fuelled her pique.

Go on, ring him. You know you want to, urged a traitorous little voice inside her. Why put it off?

Her pulse started to throb as she delved into her bag on the dressing table and with trembling hands took out the card he'd given her on the day he had driven her to the dentist. She stared at his name printed in bold type on the card, hesitating, wondering what she was going to say.

Just do it, that little voice came again, more determinedly this time, and without further hesitation she pulled herself together, taking deep steadying breaths as she waited for the number to connect.

'Jared Steele.'

Nothing could have prepared her for the enervating effect just hearing his voice would have upon her so that, unsteady on her legs, she sank down onto the boudoir chair in front of the mirror, dark lashes pressed against the well of her eyes as she struggled to cope.

'Hello?' The deep voice was overlaid with just a hint of impatience.

Taylor opened her eyes. Her cheeks were flushed and her green eyes were unusually bright in the mirror.

Praying for composure, she uttered without any preamble, 'Where have you taken my car?'

Silence at the other end of the line indicated that her preemptive demand had knocked him a little off balance. Recovering, he gave a soft chuckle. 'Is that your way of thanking me for taking the trouble to try and help you out?'

Tension increased Taylor's grip on the tiny mechanism. 'I didn't need helping out.'

'I thought you did. Leaving a damaged vehicle sitting around in this damp weather could result in a much bigger job than you bargained for if it started to rust.'

Why did men always have an answer for these things? she thought, gritting her teeth, and started as Thai, having found his way in from the roof of the outbuilding under her bathroom window, suddenly leapt up onto her lap.

'I wouldn't have let it come to that,' she stated with a hand on the cat's warm, bony back as he circled her lap and settled down. 'I was going to get it done next week. You know I've been away.' Or hadn't you noticed! she thought, her heart aching from the knowledge of what could have kept him from contacting her.

She heard his heavily sighed, 'Yes,' come over the line, imagined him in his office, lounging back in his deep leather chair in front of his desk, clean-cut, hard and dynamic. 'Well, let's just say it's a peace-offering for not keeping our date before you went off to Greece.'

'A peace-offering.' Tears stung her eyes. Were her feelings for him so hopelessly transparent that he thought he could get round her just like that? Bitterly she said, 'So what happened to the adoring Alicia? Did you manage to get rid of her without too much hassle? Or doesn't she actually mind conducting an affair with you while you still have a wife!'

She heard him take a deep breath, let it out again very slowly. 'Taylor…we have to talk.'

So this was it. Crunch time, she thought, guessing the reason for that flat, incontrovertible edge to his voice.

Something seemed to wither way down inside of her, leaving an aching void she knew would never be filled.

'OK.' It was an attempt at bravado that made her sound impervious, totally uncaring. 'So talk.'

'Not over the phone,' he demurred, and now his voice too came over as cold, like a stranger's, someone she didn't know. 'Some things can only be discussed face to face. Apart from which, I don't relish the idea of having it slammed down on me again.'

Taylor smarted from the reminder, the hurt anger that had prompted her to do it—nothing to the numbing pain she was suffering now.

'Will it be any problem to collect your car in the morning?' he asked, cutting across her attempts to tell him that she would rather talk now; that they didn't need to have to meet. She knew what he was going to say and she didn't think she could bear it!

'What?' Her numbness made her slow to follow his swift change of subject. A dull pain between her eyes promised a corker of a headache. 'Er, no.'

'Good,' he said, and it wasn't until then, playing distractedly with the tip of one warm feline ear, that she realised she was shaking. 'I'll pick you up at eight,' he concluded, and abruptly rang off.

CHAPTER ELEVEN

HE ARRIVED, as promised, punctual to the minute, his time-keeping faultless, as it had always been.

About to run downstairs and open the front door, Taylor opened hers to see Charity, still in her dressing gown and slippers and with the morning post in her hand, already letting him in.

From her vantage point at the top of the stairs, Taylor caught their exchange of pleasantries, those lazy tones of Jared's, rich and deep against the bubbly brightness of Charity's.

He was stooping to pet one of the cats that had wandered out from the downstairs flat, scratching her ears—Taylor noted it was Asia—while the animal submitted to those strong teasing fingers in obvious ecstasy, chocolate-coloured paws lifting irreverently to the immaculate dark cloth of his suit.

Then he straightened, glanced up, and all Taylor's resolve to hang on to her composure was torn to shreds as those penetrating eyes met hers.

Obviously dressed for the city, he looked hard, cool and lethal, that clean-cut executive image concealing the primeval passions of his dark and devastating sexuality.

Under the burn of his regard she felt herself growing hot, the long grey coat she had already donned with her pink scarf hanging loosely around her shoulders, suddenly far too warm in the centrally heated hall.

'Are you ready?' he asked smoothly, making no attempt to disguise his appraisal of the slash-neck pink sweater and long grey fitted skirt she wore beneath her open coat as she came downstairs.

She wanted to say no. Insist on his telling her where her car was; to say whatever it was he had to say and go, because she didn't think she could take the prolonged agony of being with him when she already had a very good idea what it was he was going to tell her.

'Yes,' she murmured, acknowledging Charity's 'good morning' and then, conceding defeat, let Jared lead her out to his car.

'How was Greece?' he wanted to know, when almost instantly they were in the thick of the rush-hour traffic, his gaze travelling briefly over her face, lightly tanned from the early Mediterranean sun.

'Fine,' she said tightly, looking out of her window, her eyes trained on a basket of bright, assorted primroses hanging outside a florist's shop.

He sent a stray glance in her direction. 'You look tired,' he said.

Because I went to bed with a headache and then I couldn't sleep, she wanted to tell him, but she didn't, her stomach knotted so tightly she didn't feel like making small talk.

Glancing at his dark, arresting profile she said rather grudgingly, 'You don't.' And with a dart of something painful arrowing through her, couldn't help tagging on, 'Has your mistress been treating you well during my absence?'

'What do you want me to say, Taylor?' He was manoeuvring the car to avoid an obstruction on their side of the road. 'What is it exactly you want to hear?'

Say, 'No! She hasn't been with me!' Say, 'I haven't seen her!' she screamed silently, only he didn't.

'I trust she got over her tummy ache!' she uttered waspishly.

'She's getting better,' he answered, checking his mirror, while she noted with painful clarity the way he had referred to the woman. As though she were still there with him, Taylor thought, anguish overriding the sudden guilty speculation that the woman's sickness might have been far less trivial than she had implied. 'She's on the road to recovery,' he was stressing, before she could question him about either point, 'but I'm not sure that we are, Taylor. All what's happened does rather beg the question that if you have such little faith in me—such lack of trust—what sort of foundation is that to try to build a marriage on?'

She had been looking at his strong, dexterous hand dealing with the gear stick and his silken-haired wrist, strikingly dark against the snowy cuff of his shirt, but now his words brought her gleaming head up with a jerk.

What was he saying? Why was he acting as though he were the injured party when she had been torn in two by his lack of concern for her? By the way he had treated her?

'Can you blame me?'

He seemed to give some consideration to this before answering. 'With anyone else I would have said "yes". With you, Taylor, who knows what's going on in that very bewildering and complex brain of yours?'

She sent a sideways look at him, her forehead puckering. 'What's that supposed to mean?'

'I mean you give the impression of being calm and in control. Self-sufficient. Self-contained. Self-deluded.' She darted him a look that contested that last uncomplimentary remark, but he ignored it, his eyes trained on the traffic ahead. 'Behind that cool exterior there's a mass of seething resentments and insecurities. Jealousy. Suspicion. You name it.'

'That's not true!'

'Isn't it?'

'No,' she defended, wondering why he kept trying to

blame her for everything when he was the one who was clearly at fault—refusing to come clean about the other woman; refusing to give her straight answers. 'Anyway, if you're so blameless in all this...you knew how upset I was. Why didn't you ring me? Before I went away? Why not, if everything's so innocent as you say?'

The glance he sliced her was harshly cynical. 'Do you really want to know?'

From the tone of his voice she had a feeling she wasn't going to like what was coming.

'I was angry—very angry, dammit! I wasn't feeling particularly conciliatory after the way you slammed the phone down on me—refused to listen. I didn't think you were in any sort of mood to be reasoned with.'

'Apart from which, you had far more pressing things on your mind!' Achingly she remembered how the following morning she had telephoned the apartment, remembered the empty silence, the answering machine that he had forgotten to switch on.

'Yes,' he said heavily. 'I did.'

Because he was with Alicia and nothing in the world was going to change that.

Tears threatening to betray her, she forced herself nevertheless to say steadily, 'We didn't have to meet up like this. There was no reason to,' she complained, hurting more with each passing second that she had to sit there beside him. 'Why can't you leave me alone?'

'Is that what you really want?'

'You know it is.'

'Then I had some pretty conflicting messages up there in Cumbria.'

'That was different,' she argued, feeling the heat creeping up her throat and into her face from the memory of their wild, uninhibited lovemaking. 'It wasn't a normal situation. We were forced together. It wasn't real.'

'Really?' His eyes were hard as he glanced across at her. 'Well if that wasn't real, dearest, then I'm afraid I've been guilty of some pretty decadent fantasies.'

'You know what I mean!' With a lift of her chin Taylor turned away from those glitteringly dark eyes, the action emphasising the fine symmetry of her delicate bone structure. She didn't want to remember. Why was he doing this? 'It doesn't alter the fact,' she argued painfully, 'that I could have picked the car up myself. You didn't need to see me.'

'Didn't I?' Above the monotonous rhythm of the indicator his tone was clipped, and his jaw was set in a grim cast as he manoeuvred the powerful car to take a right-hand turn. 'Do you really think after what happened that first night we were snowed up together, I'd just walk away without at least checking to see if there had been any... repercussions?'

Of course. She should have thought of that. 'You mean am I pregnant?' she enquired flatly, for some crazy moment almost wishing she was, managing somehow not to reveal the depth of anguish she felt inside.

A darkly clad shoulder lifted in the briefest of shrugs.

'No,' she answered, chancing a glance at him now.

Was he relieved? She couldn't tell—couldn't read anything from his expression because the bright morning sunlight, broken by the buildings they were passing, was chasing hard shadows across his face. His jaw though was thrust out as though against some inner battle with himself and when she looked at those capable hands again they were surprisingly white-knuckled as they gripped the wheel.

He didn't say anything after that and wearily Taylor's head dropped back against the headrest, her disturbed and broken night's sleep taking its toll.

Apart from when they had been together up in Cumbria, there had always been so many doubts and uncertainties threatening their marriage—so many pressures dominating their lives. Social pressures. His job. Hers. Yet, for a while, marooned up there above that snow-bound valley, lost in each other, nothing else had seemed to matter. They had become so close for a while. As close, she could have believed, as it was possible for two human beings to get. But then that phone call from Steve that last morning had killed it all with such cruel and merciless finality, resurrecting the old threats and insecurities. But was it all her fault, as Jared would have her believe? Were all these doubts just figments of her imagination? Because if they were, why wasn't he telling her so? Why was he so ready to let her believe that he didn't care?

The sound of the car slowing down to stop at a junction brought her eyes flickering open.

'I thought you were asleep,' Jared commented.

'No.' She sat up now, peering out at unfamiliar, suburban streets. Unfamiliar and yet… 'Where are we?' A frown drew her fine brows together. Seeing the name of the locality above a small grocery store, however, she looked at him questioningly, uttered an uncertain little laugh. 'Wasn't this rather a long way to bring my car?'

'There's something I need to do—I think you need to do,' he said softly, 'before I take you to the garage.'

'What?' Her green eyes were glittering warily and her words were tinged with suspicion. 'Where are we going?'

He didn't answer, just sat there like a relentless tormentor, steering the big car along the wide carriageway while her heart beat with increasing rapidity.

Across the road was the park. Yes, that was it. And the stone wall on this side…

She remembered the wall. It had seemed so high, but it wasn't. It wasn't high at all.

A long-forgotten despair seemed to clutch at her chest and, even as she was visualising the gap in the wall, Jared was turning the car in through a pair of gateless stone pillars onto the driveway of the small stone manor house.

The front garden looked unkempt, with straggling bushes and shrubs and there were bags of cement and sand stacked around one side of the house. It appeared to be unoccupied, Taylor noted, frowning, and there was a sign for a renovation company propped up against one of the walls.

Conscious of the car coming to a halt, the glance she shot Jared was guarded, almost accusing.

'Why did you bring me here?' she asked tremulously, and then, with a jerk of her chin towards the empty building, feigning ignorance, she tagged on, 'What's this supposed to be?'

A crease brought those thick masculine eyebrows together. Softly Jared said, 'Don't you know?'

Tension etched deeply into her fine features, Taylor turned sharply away. The next instant she was pushing her door open, getting out of the car.

She stopped near the edge of a stretch of patchy earth that had once been a lawn, looking towards the tall conifers that hemmed it on the other side. There was still a small worn rectangle of paved ground in front of them, she noted poignantly, where the swings used to be.

'This is where your father left you, isn't it, while he went to look for your mother?' The deep voice coming unexpectedly from behind her made Taylor stiffen, although she didn't turn around. 'Every time she left you both. Ran away.'

She sucked in her breath. 'How did you find out?'

'I made a few enquiries. I also telephoned your mother.'

Incredulity showed in the eyes she turned his way.

'Oh, she wasn't too forthcoming,' he said tightly. 'Not at first. She came around a bit after a while. What she left unsaid, I pieced together.'

Turning away from him, holding her voice steady, she remarked, 'You've been busy.'

'I just wanted to know the truth,' he said. 'I knew that your parents had split up, and that you didn't appear to have been unduly affected by it when you told me. Recently though, I felt there had to be something more.'

She made a soft sound down her nostrils. 'Clever, astute Jared.' She sent a bitter, brief glance in his direction. 'There really isn't very much that escapes you, is there? What made you wonder?'

'I'm not really sure. There was always that hard-shell attitude around children—even to any discussion of the subject. But I'd seen how you were with Josh. I saw you that day in that car park when that little girl thought she'd lost her mother. You looked as though something was tearing you to shreds. I thought it was because—'

When he didn't finish, she supplied, 'Because you thought I'd got rid of ours?' The knowledge that he could think such a thing still hurt unbearably, like something twisting deep down inside of her.

She heard the ragged breath he expelled which sprang, she knew, from deep, self-castigating regret. 'Then there was that vociferous little lamb you nearly broke both our necks over when we were away. You were much too affected for it to have been simply concern for an animal's welfare. I needed to know.'

She turned around, looking towards the house, seeing it, not as the developer's dream it was now, but as it was before—a home for lost, abandoned and unhappy little souls. 'You could have asked.'

'Would you have told me?'

She didn't answer—knew he wasn't expecting her to. Instead, distantly she murmured, 'That first time...she just didn't bother to come home. Someone always walked me home from school—left me at the door—an older girl—but when I knocked that day, there was no one there. My father worked late and wasn't due home until nearly midnight. He left work early that day, I'm not sure why, but he did. It was the dead of winter and I'd been outside the house for nearly two hours. A couple of the neighbours knew because they'd spoken to me as they were passing. "Mummy won't be long", they said and let themselves into their lovely warm houses—' her voice was strung with the hurt anger and disbelief such adult apathy still aroused in her '—but no one took me in even though I was crying and it was bitterly cold. Can you believe that! There weren't any other relatives—no one,' she repeated, 'so my father brought me here. He had to work, you see, as well as try to find my mother.'

'She found out he was having an affair,' Jared commented, 'and to punish him she left her five-year-old daughter out in the snow.' The harshness of his tone told Taylor exactly what he thought about that.

'It wasn't like that,' Taylor uttered quickly, leaping to her mother's—both her parents'—defence. 'She had problems. I suppose you could call her unstable and sometimes I think my father's life was pretty unbearable. I don't suppose I could blame him for falling in love with someone else. She was his childhood sweetheart—a girl he knew before my mother. I think he wanted to do the right thing and give her up, but I suppose he couldn't. But he couldn't leave my mother either. I think he was worried about what would become of me if he had. I think—no, I *know*—that was the only reason he stayed.' Because he hadn't wanted to risk losing custody of his little girl and the inseparable bond that had formed between them.

Feeling emotion welling up inside her, Taylor turned and moved across the worn lawn.

There were crocuses, she noted, dotted here and there, their purple heads sagging, going over now, but the small clumps of miniature daffodils were only just bursting forth, golden trumpets bobbing in the keen breeze, heralding another year, another spring.

'I suppose I was never here for more than a few days each time,' she reflected aloud, aware of Jared striding beside her across the grass. 'But that seems like an eternity when you're a child. Eventually when I was about twelve, Mum left for good and I stayed with my father then until he died.'

'And his ladylove?'

'She got tired of waiting and married someone else.'

The silence that stretched away on the cool breeze, penetrated only by the liquid notes of a thrush high in one of the conifers, made her wonder if he was thinking what she was. That it seemed a similar scenario to the one she had accused him of acting out after what she had overheard being said on the balcony of his apartment that night, so long ago now.

'And you were—how old when he died?' Jared asked, glancing at her. 'Fifteen?'

'Yes.'

'When you went to live with your mother and her partner.' She remembered telling him that much when they were first going out together. She nodded, and realised that something of her feelings must have shown on her face because sagaciously he was adding, 'You didn't like that very much.'

Hands deep in her coat pockets, she had stopped by the rectangle of tarmac and was looking down at it with long-buried emotion clouding her eyes.

When she spoke even to her own ears she sounded like someone very small and lost. 'I'd never felt so abandoned in my life.'

She hadn't got on with her stepfather, and not particularly well with her mother. She had always felt her mother's new partner resented her intrusion into their lives.

'They both drank and then would start shouting abuse at me and at each other. I was often the butt for their frustrations, and my schoolwork began to suffer. Sometimes I was so unhappy, I just couldn't face any classes. Some people think truancy's a lark—a skiving off school for the sheer hell of it—and perhaps it is for a lot of kids. But for some it's just substituting one misery for another. There's not much fun to sitting in the park, with no food or money, cold, hungry and miserable, when all you want to do is go home.'

The look she gave Jared was almost defensive, as though she were half expecting him to challenge her statement. But the bright sunlight was making his eyes gleam like dark sherry and in them she read both sympathy and understanding.

Of course, she remembered after a moment. He might have had a loving home with his grandparents, but he'd felt the lack of a mother's love in spite of that.

'I tried to make a go of it,' she said emphatically, trying to convince herself as much as Jared, 'even when Mum refused to let me finish my education and she took me out of school. Neither of them worked you see, so I tried to do what she wanted—help them both out—to earn some money. But I couldn't take their continual quarrelling on top of being made to feel that I was only wanted for what I could contribute, and one day I just left.'

She could still hear her mother's shrill anger berating her after the first attempt to leave her unhappy environment had been foiled and her whereabouts disclosed by the well-meaning friend with whom she had been staying.

'I know you think I deserted your father, but he deserved it. Anyway you're more like me than you realise—only worse. You can't stick at anything. You'll run away from every situation as soon as things aren't to your liking', the woman had rammed home, reminding Taylor of her truancy, her first hated job on the supermarket check-out she had lost in favour of attending a local art workshop; her disregard, as her mother had put it, for any responsibility, etching on her brain those disparaging words that still haunted her today. 'You'll always run away.' But she didn't tell Jared any of that.

She was right. I'm just like her, only far, far worse, she realised wretchedly, adding to the list the fiasco of her marriage. *But at least I've had the foresight not to involve any children.*

On a self-censuring little sigh, she asked, 'Why did you have to bring me here?'

'Because I didn't think it was possible for you—for either of us—to move on until you'd confronted your past—laid a few ghosts.'

Either of us? Hope tried to surface for a second, but it was only for a second.

'Told you everything, you mean.'

'I didn't do it for my benefit.'

No, she thought. Because how could it benefit him when he wasn't going to be around? Because he wasn't. She could see it in his expression. In that shuttered look in his beautiful dark eyes.

With lines corrugating his forehead, rather raggedly he was demanding, 'Why didn't you ever trust me enough to *talk* to me?'

She gave a defensive little shrug. 'Shame, I suppose, for one thing. It's true what they say. Children always blame themselves when things go wrong in a marriage. For another—you were always so busy—so tied up with your work.'

'Was I?' His sigh was self-condemnatory. 'I suppose I never took into account how inexperienced you were—how much younger you are than I am. That you needed far more time and attention than I gave you. It was my fault for not recognising how insecure you were.' His use of the past tense had an ominous ring to it.

Shivering, pushing back strands of hair that a playful wind was tugging across her face, she said, 'So now you know.'

His eyes scanned the fine contours of her face as though seeing her for the very first time. 'Now I know.'

And it wasn't a pretty picture, she thought. The character it painted.

Uttering a tight little laugh, she asked, 'So where do we go from here?'

His eyes were still searching hers, trying to penetrate the taut beautiful mask of her features to the real woman she was determined to keep him from seeing. 'Can we go any-where?' he asked sombrely.

Of course. He had said that they had no foundation on which to rebuild their marriage, she thought, and could only shrug, hurting so much that she was unable to plead with him to let them try and start again, unable to speak.

'You've got a lot of sorting out to do, Taylor, and it isn't anything anyone else can do for you. In the meantime, I will respect your wishes—leave you alone as you sug-gested,' he said. 'Accept that the decision you made over a year ago was the right one. For you...' a breath inflated his chest, held it rigid for a moment, then caused it to fall again '...for me. It was wrong of me to try and make you see things differently.'

Another sigh shuddered through his chest, and he looked suddenly bleak, she thought wonderingly, until she realised that, of course, he would have regrets.

'It might not be me, but one day someone's going to come along you're going to trust enough to want to share his life—maybe have his children. Oh, yes, you will,' he averred, seeing her shaking her head in staunch denial. How could he know that what she was denying with such heart-rending anguish was his suggestion that she could ever love anyone else when she knew she would always be in love with him? That no other man could ever take his place?

'You want everything to be safe and certain, but life isn't like that, Taylor.' A sudden gust, whipping up across the fir trees made her shiver violently, though it was more from the cold isolation she was feeling rather than the chilling wind. He reached around her, his long fingers unfolding the scarf, pulling it up over the bright sheen of her hair. 'Life's a gamble,' he whispered, those strong hands—suddenly cupping the soft fabric around her face—so surprisingly tender that the gesture brought emotion welling into her eyes. 'Oh, I don't advocate unnecessary risks but you have to at least take a chance. If you don't, you miss out on so much—so many things you shouldn't be deprived of. If you play it too safe—refuse to be governed by your true feelings—like trusting—having the children you want you'll—' He paused for a fraction of a second. 'What was it Gibran said? "Laugh, but not all of your laughter, and weep…"' His broad thumb moved lightly across her cheek, brushing away the streak of moisture evoked by his tenderness.

'But not all of my tears?' Huskily she paraphrased the work of the poet he had been quoting—a mystical work, she remembered, which they had both once agreed contained some of the most beautiful language ever written. 'That was from his chapter on love,' she reminded him, swallowing emotion, guessing he would think it sprang from reliving her past. 'Not children.'

He shrugged, his lips compressing. 'It amounts to pretty much the same thing.'

What was he saying? That she didn't love him—had never really loved him enough? Didn't he know that she was dying inside from the knowledge that she might never see him again? The hopeless comprehension that it might not be Alicia, but solely her own doubts and suspicions that had driven him away?

'I'm sorry,' she murmured, not knowing how she was going to bear it, not realising how conclusive it sounded when she tagged on, 'for everything.'

A shadow seemed to flit across that handsome face, reminding her for a few seconds of the wild man of the fell who had lived for the moment, taking her to the heights of joy, excitement and sensuality in equal measure so that suddenly she wanted to cry out, *Don't go! Don't leave me! I'll be anything you want me to be, only don't leave me like this!*

For one heart-stopping second she thought he had heard her silent pleas; sensed such a suppressed intensity of emotion in him that she thought he was about to reach for her, wanted to reach for him, blurt out without any reservation just how much she loved him.

But then a car horn blared in the street beyond the grounds and the moment was lost for ever.

'Come on,' he said and his voice sounded thick and husky. 'Let's go and get your car.'

CHAPTER TWELVE

PICKING up her empty mug, Taylor carried it through into the impeccably tidy kitchen, the uncluttered shelves and work surfaces bringing to mind something Jared had said that first night in Cumbria; something about her liking for order sometimes being infuriating.

What was it he had said exactly as he'd picked up her used mug from the hearth? That had she been back home, it would have been in the dishwasher before it was even cold?

With her fingers hooked around the door release catch of the appliance, she paused, realising she was doing exactly what he had accused her of doing, until, in sudden defiance of herself, she dumped the still-warm mug down on the draining board, and walked away, taking an almost guilty pleasure from leaving it there.

Mess up your hair. Rough it for a while. Wasn't that what he had advised her to do? In other words be less rigid, she interpreted, coming back into the immaculate sitting room.

Well, that was easily rectified, she thought, as the soulless perfection of her surroundings seemed to scream at her and, with a sudden tightening of her lips, she picked up a scatter cushion from one of the sofas and shied it across the room, closely followed by another, then snatching up two more from the opposite settee, sent those flying in the same fashion.

Catching sight of herself in the mirror hanging above the fireplace, she tugged her T-shirt out of the waistband of her jeans and ruffled her hair into a tousled mess.

'There, Jared Steele! Is that untidy enough for you?' she uttered through teeth clenched in self-rebellion, tears burning her eyes as she flopped hopelessly down on to one of the sofas.

You want everything to be safe and certain, but life isn't like that. Life's a gamble...

Wasn't that what he had said that day, over a month ago, when he had forced her to confront her past?

She had never really looked too closely at herself until then, but ever since she had been thinking a lot about what he had said and now it was as though she were seeing herself for the first time, and she wasn't sure she liked what she saw.

Perhaps she played everything too safe, she thought. Possibly it was for the same reason that she was so fastidiously tidy. Probably the psychologists would say that it was some deep-rooted need to redress the balance, a craving for order after the insecurity and chaos of her childhood. But was it asking for too much to want the man you loved to love you? To ache every day with the need to hear from him—see him again? And yet he hadn't contacted her since that day they had collected her car from the garage, when she had watched him walk across that forecourt, back to his own saloon, and she'd driven away with a newly repaired car and a heart that was broken in two.

So many times over the past month she had thought about ringing him; telling him she had been wrong not to trust him; that she loved him—wanted to be with him, but she still harboured so many doubts. Like, why had he let her go if there was no one else in his life, as his anger with her and everything he had said that last day seemed to indicate? Had he been telling her the truth, as she so desperately wanted to believe? In which case, would he welcome hearing from her? Or had her jealousy and suspicions finally destroyed what feeling he had been trying to nurture between them again? Maybe he had just simply stopped loving her?

Tears flowed unchecked as she considered that it might all have been her own fault that he had chosen finally to walk away from her. And yet he had been so gentle that last day. So infinitely tender...

She must have nodded off, worn down by the see-saw of her emotions, hearing from somewhere in her semi-consciousness the distant ring of the doorbell in the flat below.

Tired as she was, she must have gone straight back to sleep because the next thing she was aware of was the peal of her own doorbell.

Charity! she realised, remembering that it was Friday and that her friend always brought up some of the Eve's Pudding she baked for her family on a Friday night.

It was Charity, minus the pudding. She was standing there with another woman.

'Visitor for you,' Charity said smiling. They were both looking at Taylor rather oddly.

'Thanks,' the woman said over her shoulder to Charity who was already halfway down the stairs. Her voice was soft and just from that one word, Taylor decided, unmistakably American.

'Hi. I'm Alicia Hart. Mind if I come in?'

Flummoxed, Taylor pushed the door wider, silently appraising this slim, attractive older woman with her shoulder-length dark hair who, even with high-heeled shoes complementing the casual trouser suit she wore, was still several inches shorter than Taylor. A light floral fragrance followed her in.

'So you're the woman who came over here thinking she could claim my husband?' Taylor's stomach, as she closed the door, seemed to be screwed into a tight ball.

'May I sit down?' The woman indicated a sofa, sent a

rather questioning glance over Taylor and when Taylor, still too stunned too respond, said nothing, took her silence as affirmation. 'You didn't lose Jared to me, Taylor. You did that for yourself. You couldn't hang on to him even when you'd been given the chance.'

'I beg your pardon?' Now that she had recovered her senses, angrily Taylor faced the woman square on.

Was Alicia accusing her of taking him away from her? Was that why she had come? she wondered. For a show-down? Or had she turned up there simply to gloat?

'I know it's got to seem presumptuous…' frowning, the woman lifted her gaze from the cushions strewn across the floor '…but I just couldn't go back to the States without paying a call.'

Oh, couldn't she? Crossing the room, Taylor swooped down and gathered up the offending cushions. 'Why?'

'To tell you how things were.' An element of uncertainty had crept into the woman's voice before she added emphatically, 'Are.'

'I really don't think—' *I need to know this*, Taylor was about to say, tossing the four cushions onto the unoccupied settee, but broke off as she suddenly caught sight of herself in the mirror and was shockingly reminded that she had done more than fling cushions around before Charity had rung her bell.

Her T-shirt was hanging half out of her jeans, and from the state of her hair she looked as though she had been wired up to the mains! No wonder both women had been looking at her so strangely, she thought, when she had opened the door!

'I can't deny I was in love with Jared,' the woman was continuing as Taylor, determined to brazen it out, decided nevertheless that she'd be less conspicuous if she sat down.
Was?

'And I don't think anyone could blame me. He's not the

type of man any woman can ignore, is he? But I didn't come here to tell you that.'

'Just exactly why have you come here, Alicia?' Taylor wasn't sure where she was getting her strength from to challenge the woman like this. Even so, her attack approach didn't appear to faze the older woman.

'When Jared called me—the day he came back from his vacation—I was in pretty bad shape,' she said. 'I was incapable of doing anything for myself and Jared found himself having to bear the brunt of it. He took me back with him to his apartment—tried to help all he could—but I'm afraid I landed him with a whole heap more trouble than he'd bargained for. Neither of us dreamed how serious the poisoning was, but the following morning I was in the hospital.'

'The hospital?' So that was what Jared had meant when he'd responded to her accusation about having a lot on his mind, Taylor realised. And all the time she had thought…

'They kept me in longer than I expected. When I was discharged I was still not fit enough to look after myself and if it hadn't been for Jared…' She broke off, making an expressive little gesture with her hands.

'You stayed with him.'

'Yes, but—'

'At the apartment.'

'For a while.'

Taylor closed her eyes. She didn't want to hear this.

But the woman went on regardless. 'He did everything for me—I had no one else you see—but things aren't at all like you think.'

Taylor fixed her with guarded green eyes, noting how blue her rival's were, blue and big beneath thick, but well-defined dark eyebrows. 'How do you know what I think? Feel?' she queried acidly.

'Probably the worst—because I don't think Jared will

have told you all the facts,' the soft accented voice surprised her by saying. 'His code as a gentleman probably wouldn't permit it.'

A pained grimace tugged at Taylor's mouth. 'That's a rather old-fashioned term.'

'He's a rather old-fashioned guy. Surely you must know that. You're his wife. Hasn't that privilege taught you anything about him?'

Feeling in no mood to take criticism from what was—when all was said and done—Jared's mistress, heatedly Taylor said, 'Not as much as not being his wife has taught you obviously. But I'm sure you've got plans to rectify that in the near future.'

Surprisingly, Alicia ignored the barb. She fixed those blue and suddenly troubled-looking eyes on Taylor.

'When I first met him,' she said at length, 'I was unhappy and alone—having just got myself out of a relationship where I was terribly unhappy. I saw Jared and I wanted him so much I didn't want to risk losing him, so I told him I was already divorced. By the time I came clean and told him I was only separated, we were both in way too deep. Then my husband had his accident. He couldn't cope alone and I couldn't have lived with myself if I hadn't gone back to him. I wanted Jared's love—I think I'd had it for a while—but more than that he refused to give me. You know what I mean. I wanted to do what was right as a wife, but I wanted Jared as well. He said it wasn't fair to either of us—or to—' She didn't have to spell it out. 'Well, you know how principled he is! He wanted a clean break—tried to tell me so many times that it was for the best—but I was terribly selfish and I clung to him. When I looked like losing him, I tried to keep him in my life using guilt.'

'Guilt?' Taylor echoed, frowning.

'I told him that the situation I was in—that my husband's accident—was his fault—both our faults—because I'd told

Roger I had a lover only minutes before he crashed that car, but it wasn't true. I just couldn't bear the thought of Jared getting involved with anyone else—being with anyone else—when I knew that if circumstances had been different, I could have been the one with him. And then he found you. From that day on I knew I'd lost him.'

Stunned, Taylor asked, 'Why are you telling me this?'

'I nearly ruined his life,' Alicia was admitting startlingly. 'Don't you do it to him too.'

Unable to believe she was sitting there listening to the woman she had always believed to be her rival, advising her in such a way, Taylor caught her breath.

'Jared loves you,' the woman went on. 'I know. A man like that's got a lot of pride. He doesn't let his feelings show too much but I know he never felt for me what he feels for you. When I heard you and he had split, I thought he might come around, contact me, but he didn't, and I wanted to contact him, but Steve... You know Steve Shaunessy?' she interjected, and without waiting for an answer, 'I met him a few times when I was dating Jared, and I used to ring him after we split to find out how his boss was doing, but he warned me off. He said how cut up Jared was over everything. How he was working too hard—how he did nothing *but* work. Oh, I know his mother was ill and he was spending a lot of time with her, but I knew it was you he was hurting over—knew he wouldn't welcome me back in his life.'

'So why did you come here?' For what other reason than to claim what was hers because she was suddenly free to do so?

'To tell him the truth face to face—what I couldn't tell him any other way. That he was in no way to blame for my husband's accident—indirectly or otherwise. Roger never knew there was anyone else in my life. His car just skidded on a muddy road. That was all.'

And all this time, Jared had been made to feel in some way responsible, Taylor realised, sympathising, remembering how bleak he had looked sometimes whenever the other woman's name was mentioned. She'd thought it was because he wanted to be with Alicia. But if what the woman was saying was true—driven, Taylor guessed, by the need to get things off her chest—had what she had taken to be futile longing in Jared simply been a deep, troubling sense of guilt?

'Jared made it clear though—in the most diplomatic way—when I was sick and he took me back to his apartment—that things were over between us a long time ago. But then I knew that already. I knew I'd never stand a chance with him after you.'

'How much could you have loved him to want to hurt him that much?' Taylor rebuked, thinking of the shadow this woman had cast over her marriage and how, if Alicia hadn't deceived Jared in the first place about her marital status, he probably would never have got involved with her.

'I'm not sure it was love. It was more like obsession,' the woman was confessing. 'I don't know how any woman who's unhappily married can look at Jared and not realise—and long for—all she's been missing. That's why I lied to him. That's why I didn't want to give him up. After he married you I used to ring your apartment sometimes just to hear him answer. Sometimes I got him, but I never spoke to him. Sometimes I got you.'

And then she put the phone down, Taylor reflected, remembering those silent but harrowing phone calls when she had imagined Jared and his lost love in secret liaison with each other.

'As I said, I think I was obsessed,' the woman reiterated, 'but now, for the first time, I feel free of it—feel ready for a brand new start. After I came out of hospital, Jared packed me off to stay with Steve and his wife. He thought

it best in the circumstances. They've got another lodger
from the States. He's a nice guy and, like me, he's headed
back tomorrow. It's early days yet, but...' A shoulder
moved nonchalantly beneath the casual jacket. 'You never
know.'

As Alicia got up, Taylor wondered just how brave a face
the woman was putting on, almost able to feel for her
through her joyous realisation that Jared had never been
unfaithful to her, that Jared loved her—or had, until she'd
driven him away.

'You know...' ready to leave, Alicia paused in the doorway, that blue gaze guarded as it raked over Taylor's taller,
leaner frame '...when I found out he was getting married
and I rang and asked him what you were like he said that
you were...perfect. Like a cultured pearl. I imagined someone stiff and plastic. You know. Over-fussy with everything—never a hair out of place—and I hated you even
more. But you're not like that at all.'

It was all Taylor could do not to shudder before the
woman swept out of the flat without another word.

The old market town of Keswick was busy when Taylor
pulled into the garage to fill up the car with fuel, though
she supposed she couldn't have expected much else on a
Saturday morning.

Even leaving London at a ridiculously early hour, the
various hold-ups and road works she had encountered on
the motorway had meant it taking far longer than she had
expected to reach the Lakeland town, and for hour upon
hour she had done nothing but sit and think about Jared,
and wonder whether she was doing the right thing.

The previous night, after Alicia had left, all she had
wanted to do was to ring him. Being told by the other
woman—of all people!—how much Jared loved her and
only her had only confirmed what she had suspected for

some time and hadn't really wanted to admit to. That it was all her own fault that her marriage had failed.

Desperate to speak to him, see him, tell him she was sorry for not believing in him and to start to put everything right, she had tried in vain to reach him but he wasn't at the apartment, nor had he been answering his mobile.

She could have left a message on both numbers, but what she wanted to say to him was far too important to say over the phone. Eventually she had managed to contact Steve Shaunessy who had given her the unexpected news. Jared was in Cumbria.

'Looking to sell his property,' was the way he had put it in his usual lilting Irish. And then, as the possible situation had obviously struck him, cagily he had added, 'But you'll know about all that, I take it?'

No, she didn't, Taylor had thought, biting her lip to stifle a small cry of pain. And Jared obviously hadn't told his henchman that he was no longer in contact with his wife.

Bluffing her way through some spiel about having been on location, she had come off the phone with her thoughts in turmoil and a cold desolation snuffing out her crazy hopes as if they were candles.

If Jared was selling his Lakeland home, surely that meant only one thing? That he no longer felt any sentimental attachment to it and wanted to put everything that had happened there behind him—if not his childhood, then most certainly their marriage, what they had shared together. Her.

She couldn't let him, she had thought hectically. Not without his knowing how she really felt. Not without his first giving her a chance!

She hadn't even tried to ring him in Borrowdale, afraid of what his reaction would be if she had. He might not welcome her call; might tell her that he had made the right decision—just as he had said she had done that last morning over a month ago—and the only way to try to convince him that it was the wrong one, she thought, was to meet him face to face.

Now, pulling out of the garage, with Borrowdale only a short distance from the old Victorian town, doubts began to crowd in. Like, would he want to see her? Would he even be there? Maybe she should have rung first, she considered now that it was too late, before being so rash as to drive all this way.

Stalling for time, she parked her car in a side street and, finding a bank, needing some money, was waiting in a queue to use the cash machine when a property in the adjacent estate agent's window caught her eye.

It was Jared's house! There was no mistaking it with its three grey gables and that sloping drive!

A lump caught in her throat but then her heart sank as she read the notice that had been stuck across it. *Under Offer.*

But how could it be? she agonised. How could he sell it when it meant so much to him? To them both? After all they had shared when they had been up here together that last time?

Forgetting all about her money, something propelled her into the shop.

'That house,' she said to the girl who was coming out from behind a desk to help her—pointing to the display. 'The one in the middle. Has it definitely been sold?'

'As good as,' the girl said, smiling, giving her the answer she had been dreading. 'I think the interested party's been after it for some time. I believe the owner's at the property now if you're thinking of putting in a better offer.' The girl's widening grin said it all. She didn't have a hope. 'You'd better be quick though. He's got a cash buyer and the deal's being agreed at exactly...' She dropped a glance at her wristwatch. 'Twelve o'clock.'

Which left next to no time to get there, let alone persuade Jared that he was doing the wrong thing, Taylor thought chaotically, checking her own, and within minutes she was back in the car, taking the road out of town.

The mountains seemed to smile down on her like old friends as she met the quieter stretch of road twisting through the valley. Everything from the pale green shoots of the shrubs and trees clothing the foothills, to the flowers on the hillsides and the new brood of lambs in the pastures proclaimed, a little later here than in London, that spring had truly arrived.

The sky was a cool clear blue, and the lake, as Taylor glimpsed it now through the wooded roadside, reflected a world turned upside down.

Like hers, she thought, feeling different from the woman who had driven along this same road two months ago. Different in her thinking, different in her outlook, even in her appearance, the stringencies of her old self left behind like a load of unwanted baggage. Perhaps it was the fear of losing Jared totally that had finally brought her to her senses, she cogitated—even before Alicia had turned up last night. But for the first time in her life she was running with a positive goal in mind and she didn't intend stopping until her goal was met.

CHAPTER THIRTEEN

DRIVING uphill from the valley, Taylor had to swallow to ease the lump in her throat as she caught sight of the three familiar grey gables, but as she drew up outside the house she saw another, unfamiliar car parked there in the lane.

Jared's purchaser?

It had to be, she thought and, glancing down at the clock on the dashboard, saw that it was one minute to twelve o'clock.

She was out of her car and opening the gate in seconds.

A bearded, middle-aged man was standing at the front door, obviously waiting for someone to answer his knock. Taylor saw the door open, saw Jared step out, and her heart lurched in her breast.

All in black, in a casual shirt and corduroys, he was more striking than she could ever remember him looking, that enigmatic image in no way tempered by the strong black hair and the surprising hint of dark stubble that shaded his jaw.

Stunned by the impact of his presence, for a moment Taylor couldn't take her eyes off him. She was seeing again the untamed, awesome Jared who had driven her wild for him in that heaven of a freeze-up, made love to her, she knew now, out of pure and simple love, a love she was praying she hadn't killed with her jealousy and suspicion.

But the two men were shaking hands and as they made to go inside, she knew she couldn't just let them—let the sale go ahead without trying to stop it.

What had she to lose? Only everything, she thought, remembering what Jared had said about life being a gamble.

Well, she was ready to bet on everything—her husband, his love, their future—and in sudden panic, nerves making her sound coldly blunt, from the gate she was calling out, 'I'm afraid my husband's selling this property without my permission!'

Which, of course, he probably could, she reasoned, as both masculine heads turned in her direction. It was in his name, wasn't it? All she was hoping for, however, was the purchaser not knowing that.

'It's true!' she went on, tripping down the path, desperation making her blurt out, 'I've got the best solicitor!'

For a moment something flared in Jared's dark eyes, something she might have said was surprised pleasure if, a second later, his face hadn't turned grim and those glittering irises hadn't been viewing her with cold, almost painful contempt.

'What the devil do you think you're doing?' It passed his lips as a rasped whisper.

Life's a gamble...

'He hasn't consulted me,' she was saying quickly now to the rather ruddy-faced man whose complexion, as ʰ glanced from Taylor to Jared and back to Taylor again, ᵥ growing redder by the second. 'And has he told you about the rats? No, I don't suppose he has! But then he wouldn't, would he? The place is infested!' she lied, knowing she was going too far. But what the hell! she thought. In for a penny, in for a pound! 'But it doesn't matter,' she stressed, 'because he can't sell it without my permission anyway!'

'Rats? What's all this about?' The man turned angrily to Jared. 'No one said anything to me about rats! Nor was I told there was a dispute going on over this property.'

Jared wasn't looking at the man. His eyes were dissecting Taylor and her stomach turned over from the seething way he breathed, 'Well, it would appear that there is.'

'This isn't good enough!' The man was clearly put out.

'Do you know how much time I've invested in this—this fiasco!—trying to raise the money? You'll not hear the last of this!' he promised them both, fuming. 'I'll be back to sort this out—*and* with my solicitor!'

'Good,' Jared snarled, distinctly in no mood to be threatened. 'Better bring a good box of rat poison with you, too.'

Taylor thought the man was about to have a seizure.

'If that's your attitude, you can stick your house!' he said rudely, storming, crimson-faced, off down the path.

'So what is it, Taylor? What's dragged you all the way to Cumbria just to try and stop me selling this place as you've so effectively succeeded in doing?' Hard fingers around her elbow were bundling her inside the house. 'Is it a settlement? Is that what this highfaluting lawyer of yours has put you up to?' he demanded above the sudden angry screech of tyres in the lane. 'To bleed me of every penny I have on top of everything else you've taken from me?'

'You can't sell it! You—' *Don't want to!* she started to say as she pulled away from him into the sitting room, but was stalled by the sight that met her.

The furniture was still in place, but all the walls and surfaces had been cleared of everything they had lovingly held. Everything, she realised, except her two Lakeland drawings still hanging on each side of the chimney-breast.

'I what?' he demanded brusquely. 'Can't sell it until we've sorted out the appropriate funds? All right. If that's all that matters to you, go ahead! Name your price!'

His eyes were glacial, but the heat of his anger was as tangible as fire. This wasn't how it was supposed to go, she thought, harrowed. How she had intended it to be.

'Jared. What's happened to you? To us?'

'Was there any us?'

'You know there was.'

'Ah, yes. The obliging little siren who offered me pleasure without commitment.' His stripping regard took in her unusual appearance, so different from her normally groomed, rather conservative style. Because stepping out of the shower while it was still dark that morning, she hadn't bothered blow-drying her hair as she usually did. Instead, she had simply finger-dried it very quickly with her head upside down, so that the result was a delightful mass of wild brown waves, as relaxed as the pale blue and white check fleecy shirt she had left half-buttoned, hanging loosely over her jeans, and which offered a tantalising glimpse of pale flesh and the gentle swell of a breast. 'Is that why you've come here today looking as though you've just stepped out of my bed?' he enquired hoarsely. 'To tempt me for a bigger share of the bounty?'

'Jared, don't...' She couldn't imagine that he could really believe that. 'Do you honestly think I'd have refused to cash the money you sent me in the beginning if that was all I'd been interested in?'

He turned away, his broad back like a dark immovable door closed against her. Looking past him, her eyes fell on her two lonely sketches.

'You haven't taken my pictures down,' she commented sadly.

His shoulders stiffened beneath the soft black shirt, hard muscles locking together. 'No.'

'Why not?' Didn't he want them any more? Want to be reminded of her? Of what they had shared?

'They belong in this house.'

Had she imagined it, or had his voice trembled?

'So you're selling them with it.'

He gave a snort of what might have been derision. '*You* belong in this house!' he growled savagely. 'Or I *thought* you did.'

Behind the vehemence in his words, there was something else, something that made Taylor take a step forward.

'I still do.'

Life's a gamble…

She reached out, touched a hand to his shoulder, felt his big frame tense in rejection.

'Jared, please…'

He swung round then and so roughly that she took a step back, her hand still suspended in the air.

'What is it you want from me?' he said gutturally. With the bright day lighting the harsh angles of his strong, unshaven face he had never looked more forbidding, or more vulnerable.

It was that vulnerability that made her bold enough to respond softly, 'Anything you care to give. But I'll understand it if you've got nothing left. I know I've been unreasonable. Irrational. But I want to make it up to you, if you'll just let me.'

Head tilted to one side, his dark eyes were narrowing as though he didn't wholly believe her.

'Why the change of heart?'

'I've had time to think. And as well as that…' She hesitated, unsure for a moment whether she should tell him, but then decided she should. 'Alicia came to see me.'

'Alic—' He looked incredulous, dumbfounded. 'When?' he demanded brusquely.

'Last night.'

'She had no right,' he said.

'Perhaps she thought she owed it to you.'

'Owed it to me?' For a moment she saw his eyes darken with something she had so often mistaken for pain—the pain of wanting someone who wasn't Taylor Adams. But then as clarity dawned, he nodded, and the darkness was gone.

'She said she nearly ruined your life. But I've been far, far worse. I've wanted you so much, I couldn't believe that I wasn't going to lose you to someone else—to her—sooner or later. The thought of you with her just festered until I couldn't bear it! Everyone I ever loved—I lost—eventually. I couldn't believe that it wasn't going to happen with you.'

'Oh, my love!'

One stride brought him to her and on a small cry of wanting she was in his arms, welcoming the mouth that came down hungrily over hers.

For a moment it was as if the universe had exploded on one great starburst of joy, and she clung to him, hands revelling in his hard familiar warmth, head falling back in wild acceptance of his devouring kisses over her cheek, her jaw, her throat.

'I didn't know how you could believe that I could want another woman after knowing what you do to me—what you've always done to me,' he said raggedly. 'That was why I was so angry when you wouldn't listen to me—when I tried to tell you I couldn't leave Alicia in the state she was in. Call it pride if you like, but I was half hoping you'd have second thoughts and ring me. When you hadn't by the following morning I thought you obviously still doubted everything I'd said, and I couldn't believe it. Couldn't accept that no matter how upset you were by being robbed of our last evening together, you wouldn't have reasoned it out after a few hours and realised that I couldn't possibly be unfaithful to you—love anyone else—particularly after that wonderful week we'd just spent together.'

Did he say *love*?

Suddenly the world seemed to be turning on its axis, a wonderful joyous new world, as topsy-turvy as the reflections she had seen in the lake on the way there.

'But I did. Ring you,' she elaborated, her brow puckering from the painful memory of that morning, her palms registering the sharp rise of his heavily contoured chest beneath his shirt.

'When?'

'The following morning. But you weren't there. I thought you'd gone out with…her.'

Frowning he said, 'I was at the hospital.'

Her smile was a blend of pain and self-derision. 'I know that now. Oh, Jared, I've been so stupid. I love you. Haven't I ever told you that?'

He grimaced. 'Not for a long time.'

She gave a sheepish little shrug. 'I was afraid to commit myself.' Then, with her fingers absently slipping the buttons of his shirt, she murmured, 'Well, I do.' She heard him catch his breath as she pressed her lips to the warm, hair-roughened flesh she had exposed. 'I love you,' she whispered against the strong, hard rhythm of his heart. 'So much.'

'And do you think I don't love you?' It was almost a reprimand as he caught her in his arms again. 'I'm crazy about you. Demented. Out of my mind! How many ways can I put it?'

Tears welled in her eyes, making them shine like bright green rivers after the clouds had dispersed, leaving the sun to penetrate their pellucid depths.

'Oh, Jared!' She couldn't believe she was hearing this at last—couldn't remember a time when he had stated it with such unreserved honesty. 'Why didn't you tell me exactly how you felt?'

'I thought I was making myself clear. But I never seemed to be able to break through. Then when we met again, I was afraid of being rejected. I'd lost you once already, remember? Knowing how you were, I didn't want to do or say anything that would scare you off and put me in danger of losing you again. And yet in not saying anything, I was driving you further and further away from me. I hadn't realised until recently just how insecure you were—and how scarred you were by your childhood. I wanted to make it right for you. Protect you. I wanted to tell you that day in the grounds of that house I took you to.'

'I wish you had,' she said, her voice strung with regret for the hours, the days, the weeks they had lost apart from each other. 'I wanted you to tell me that you wanted us to be together, but you seemed so…distant—like someone I didn't know—and I couldn't bear it! I wish you'd said *something*.'

His smile was indulgent as he shook his head, said gently, 'You weren't ready to accept me then. You still seemed bent on believing that I wanted Alicia and you needed to make up your own mind about me without any further pressure on my part. I knew I'd been too demanding—overbearing even—and I felt you needed to be sure that what you weren't feeling for me wasn't just purely physical. Glorious and quite mind-blowing, it's true, but not enough on its own to build a loving, trusting relationship. And I hadn't given you much space—any space—' he appreciated with a self-deprecating grimace '—when we were up here together in February. I hadn't intended things to happen as they did. Oh, I wanted us to get back together! But it wasn't my intention to do it solely by seducing you. I was hoping to put that on hold until I'd made you care so much about me that you were begging to come back to me before I let myself into your bed, but I'm afraid, my love, that I hadn't reckoned on just how uncontrollable this physical thing between us would still be—or that I'd have such a powerful conspirator in the weather!'

Her soft laugh turned into a pleasurable groan as the physical thing he had spoken of began its delicious assault on her body, because while he had been speaking those long tapered hands had been dealing with the buttons of her shirt that weren't already unfastened, and were now parting the fleecy fabric, exposing the creamy satin that shaped her breasts.

'You're so beautiful,' he whispered in a voice hoarse from the depth of his emotions, touching his lips to the soft perfumed skin just above the lace edging of her bra.

Her back arching, Taylor closed her eyes, breathing in his familiar and very personal scent. 'Oh, Jared, I love you.'

A long tremulous breath seemed to shudder through him.

'I want you,' he whispered, but drew back suddenly, concern overriding the desire she saw in his eyes. 'I want to make love to you but I don't have any protection and I know how strongly you feel about—'

Soft fingers were pressing lightly against his lips.

'You said life was a gamble,' she reminded him gently. 'You said I wanted everything to be safe and certain and that because of it I was depriving myself of so much, and I realise now that that's exactly what I was doing. I thought that if I didn't love too much I couldn't get hurt, and that by not having any children, I was sparing them from being hurt as well. It was absurd, I know. I can see that now. But you were right that day. Life's a balance of laughter and tears and I want to share them all with you. With our children. Through our children. Because I do want a baby— your baby. I want it more than anything else in the world. Well, after you,' she murmured with a coy smile.

'Do you really mean that?' Jared's eyes were searching hers as though trying to see beyond the clear sincerity shining in them. 'Because I wouldn't want you to feel pressured—or ever to be as unhappy again as you were before.'

Running her hand lovingly over his shoulder, Taylor smiled at the depth of his concern.

'I made myself unhappy by not being able to see that I had everything,' she told him with hard self-censure, 'and I know I was afraid of conceiving. But you don't know how tortured I was when I lost our baby. I thought it had somehow sensed all the negative thoughts I had had towards it and that was why it didn't want to survive.'

'Oh, Taylor!' He was pulling her hard against him, his words torn from the depths of his soul. 'And then I as good as accused you of being responsible for losing it.'

'It was a natural assumption,' she accepted quietly, wanting to ease his pain, 'in view of how I was.'

'No it wasn't. It was cruel and callous and I want to spend every day of my life making it up to you—if you'll let me. Will you, Taylor?'

'You just try and stop me,' she murmured against his shoulder.

'In that case...' He slipped his hand into his shirt pocket, pulled out the tiniest white leather pouch.

'My wedding ring!' she breathed amazed as he tipped the slim gold band out onto his palm.

'I brought it with me when we were here last. I was determined—and conceited enough,' he interjected with a degree of self-censure, 'to think I'd have it back on your finger by the end of that week. When we left that day after...well you know...that phone call, I left it behind because I was planning to bring you back here to propose to you again. When I packed up the final things this morning, I couldn't simply store it away in a trunk with everything else. Like your pictures. I thought that once I'd taken them down that would have been it. It would have been like accepting that it was over between us for ever—finished— final—and I just couldn't do it.'

Tears shone in her eyes as she held out her left hand and he slipped the little band back on her finger. It fitted so well there, felt so right.

'You aren't really selling this place, are you?' In spite of her happiness, regret was an ache inside her as she glanced round at the bare surfaces and empty walls.

'Are you saying you don't want me to?'

'After all the lengths I went to to try and stop you?' She looked at him incredulously, her hands moving of their own volition inside his shirt, her eager fingers exploring the warm velvet of his shoulders, his smooth hard biceps, the crisp textured hair of his chest. 'Are you kidding!'

'Ah, yes,' he reflected, the sudden sensual movement of his mouth promising all sorts of delicious retribution. 'The rats.'

'Well you said life was a gamble,' she reminded him again, excitement building inside of her, 'and I just decided I was going to put my money on the best horse in the race.'

'Quite adventurous,' he murmured, dipping his head to claim her mouth again, arousing her with the knowledge of his own arousal, with the familiar deft touch of his wonderful hands.

'Not really.' She gave a pleasurable little moan, moving to make it easier for him as his fingers moved to caress the firm warm mound of one breast. 'I already have reason to believe that he's a remarkable stud,' she breathed with a tantalising smile, 'and I'm betting on a certainty that, with my choice, I'll always come first.'

'You'd better believe it,' he responded, groaning, because having pulled his shirt out of his waistband, her hands were travelling with provocative sensuality down over the sleek smooth surface of his back. 'In fact I'm going to spend a lifetime proving it to you.' He caught his breath, as though what she was doing to him was far too pleasurable to endure. 'Whereas that first point...' Suddenly he was scooping her up into his arms, bringing love and joy and excitement bubbling over inside of her. 'The bit about the stud...' a wicked smile crinkled the lines around his eyes as he carried her towards the stairs '...I can certainly prove to you now!' he stated laughingly.

A family of dunnocks were hopping around under the winter jasmine bush, their comical twitchy movements atoning for their dull, insignificant plumage.

'Bird!' the toddling Josh pointed out to Taylor who was relaxing on a garden chair near the remainder of last season's logs.

'Yes, I can see them,' she smiled, wondering if one of the parent birds might be the same one she had seen hopping about in the snow under the same bush over two years ago.

'They managed to hatch all their own eggs this year,' she commented, this time to Jared who was standing beside her, looking contentedly out over the valley through his binoculars. The previous year a cuckoo had got into the nest and destroyed all their eggs, laying her own there, before flying off and abandoning it to the unsuspecting dunnocks. 'And talking of eggs...'

'You aren't hungry again, are you?' he asked, laughing down at her, reminding her of the ravenous appetite she seemed to have developed since they had arrived there over a week ago. Taking a spring break. Inviting Craig and Charity. 'It must be all this clean mountain air!'

'Very probably,' Taylor laughed back, reaching for the fifteen-month-old Casey, hauling him up onto her lap. 'Although...' Absently she smoothed back her son's dark hair with a loving hand. 'I did once hear someone say I'd conceive every time you sneezed.'

'Who said...' His words tailed off, incredulity lighting his beautiful dark eyes. 'You mean...'

'Confirmed this morning,' she crowed, glad that she didn't have to talk her way round the origin of the remark she had heard all those years ago at that fateful party.

In the lane, on the other side of the house, a car was pulling up. Craig and Charity, she realised, returning from Keswick and their mission to buy Craig some new walking boots.

'Do they know?' Jared whispered, as if they could possibly overhear.

'Of course not. Not yet,' Taylor assured him, guessing he must think she had confided the news to Charity when, leaving the two of them to bask in the unseasonably warm spring sunshine, he had gone out on one or two challenging treks with Craig.

'Then we'll all celebrate together,' he decided, grabbing little Josh who had been about to charge at the feeding dunnocks, lifting him high, squealing with glee, into his arms.

'You and I are going in search of some champagne,' he said conspiratorially to the toddler, as amazingly paternal towards the little boy, Taylor thought—noting the flecks of grey that had appeared in his sideburns over the past year—as he was to his own son. 'Or in your case, Mrs Steele, sparkling water.' He gave her one of those secret, private winks—the type that always made her stomach flip—as he turned to go inside. 'Don't run away.'

Like last year's cuckoo?

Like...

Watching his retreat, she closed her mind to any negative thoughts, feeling the chubby arms of the infant who was bouncing on her lap, suddenly tighten possessively around her neck.

She laughed, hugging him close to her—close to the new life that was growing inside of her—and, with her lips against the baby-soft hair, huskily she whispered, 'I won't.'